Well, if Mama had never had molasses as a little girl in Scotland and she had lived to sing about it, Charlotte knew she could do without molasses now. But this war was confusing! Until tonight, it had never had anything to do with her life, but now, it had taken all the molasses from Boston Harbor. It was unsettling to think that something happening so far away could change things right on her dinner table.

By Cynthia Rylant:

OLD TOWN IN THE GREEN GROVES
Laura Ingalls Wilder's
Lost Little House Years

The Rose Years
Laura's daughter, born 1886
LITTLE HOUSE ON ROCKY RIDGE

LITTLE HOUSE
BY BOSTON BAY

by MELISSA WILEY

HarperTrophy®
An Imprint of HarperCollins*Publishers*

Special thanks to Amy Edgar Sklansky for her invaluable help in researching the history and customs of nineteenth-century Roxbury, Massachusetts. The author also wishes to acknowledge the contributions of Chris Messier and the costumed interpreters at Old Sturbridge Village, and of Jack Larkin, Director of Research, Collections, and Library at Old Sturbridge Village and author of The Reshaping of Everyday Life.

Little House by Boston Bay

Library of Congress Cataloging-in-Publication Data
Wiley, Melissa.
    Little house by Boston Bay / Melissa Wiley. — 1st abridged ed.
        p.   cm.
Summary: An abridged version of the story of six-year-old Charlotte Tucker, who would grow up to become the grandmother of Laura Ingalls Wilder, and who feels the effects of the War of 1812 while living with her family near Boston.
    ISBN-10: 0-06-114828-8 (pbk.) — ISBN-13: 978-0-06-114828-6 (pbk.)
    1. Tucker, Charlotte—Juvenile fiction. [1. Tucker, Charlotte—Fiction. 2. Wilder, Laura Ingalls 1867–1957—Family—Fiction. 3. Family life—Massachusetts—Roxbury (Boston)—Fiction. 4. Massachusetts—History—War of 1812—Fiction. 5. United States—History—War of 1812—Fiction.] I. Title.
PZ7.W64814Lh 2007   2006103557
[Fic]—dc22   CIP
                                                                  AC

14 15 16   CG/OPM   10 9 8 7 6 5 4
❖
First Harper Trophy Edition, 1999
Abridged Harper Trophy edition, 2007

For Kate and Erin

CONTENTS

THE SATURDAY FAMILY   1

THE CORBIE AND THE CROW   10

SPRING   24

IN THE GARDEN   34

THE ROAD TO SCOTLAND   47

GREAT HILL   59

ON SCHOOL STREET   66

C IS FOR COACH   77

EMMELINE   84

POUNDED CHEESE   96

IN THE SMITHY   108

APPLE TIME   116

THE SEAGULL   127

THE SATURDAY FAMILY

Through the window, Charlotte could see Papa and the boys walking across the road from the smithy. In a moment, Mama would say, "Time to get these beans on the plate, Charlotte." Baked beans were part of the special supper that belonged to Saturday night.

Most evenings supper was simply a cold tea of bread and cheese and leftovers, for the big meal of the day was dinner, at noon. Mama seldom cooked at night—except on Saturdays.

Saturday night supper meant thick pools of cornmeal pudding on the plates beside the baked beans. It meant coffee for Mama and Papa instead of cider. And it meant three things in the middle of the dinner table—the three members of what Charlotte thought of as the "Saturday family." There was the mother, a tall, delicately curved cruet of cider vinegar for the vegetables; the father, a squat redware molasses jug with a jaunty handle and a friendly chip on the rim; and between them, cradled in a china dish, the butter baby for Mama's rolls.

Charlotte had never told anyone about the Saturday family—it was nice to have a secret all her own. Besides, she knew her brothers would tease her about it. Lewis would tease because he was a teasing kind of person, and Tom, who was seven, would tease because he wanted to be like Lewis. Charlotte's older sister Lydia never teased, but she would either be not at all interested in the secret or, worse, much *too* interested. She would take over the game and change it. To Charlotte, the Saturday family was perfect just as it was.

From the lean-to came the splashing, jostling sound of the boys washing up.

Charlotte could hear Papa and Lewis talking about the war. She had been listening to war talk almost her whole life, for the war with England had begun way back in 1812, when she was only a little girl. She knew it had something to do with sea battles, and a place called Canada way to the north, and that Mama thought it was a foolish thing and spoke of it scornfully as "Mr. Madison's War."

But when Papa came inside, smelling of coal smoke and horses, the talk of the war ended. He went to the hearth and kissed the back of Mama's neck below her white linen cap. Mama turned and smiled her special Papa-smile that made her eyes crinkle into crescent moons.

Papa tugged Lydia's thick red braids to say hello, and he stretched out one of Charlotte's dark ringlets like a spring. Then he bent down to baby Mary, who was playing with a rolling pin on the floor at Mama's feet, and swept her up into his arms. This was the Saturday night that Charlotte loved. Carrying the breadboard, she followed Lydia and her brothers along the narrow hallway, past the stairs and the front door, into the parlor for supper.

Soon Mama came into the parlor, tucking wisps of her red hair back into place beneath her cap, and just behind her was Papa, with Mary in his arms.

Charlotte listened to the fire pop and sigh beneath the sound of Papa's quiet voice as he spoke the words of the blessing. Then Papa said, "Amen," and that was when Charlotte opened her eyes and realized at once that something was not right.

The Saturday father was missing. The vinegar mother was there in her usual place, and the fat, dimpled lump of butter was beside her in its little china crib. But the jolly redware jug wasn't there.

Before Charlotte could say anything, Lewis noticed it, too. "Lydia forgot the molasses for our pudding!" he announced. It was one of the few chores of Lydia's that Charlotte longed to do.

"I did not either forget!" Lydia protested. "There isn't any molasses. Right, Mama?"

"Aye," Mama said. "You ought to be careful about letting your tongue set sail without a compass, Lewis." She winked at him and everyone laughed, because that was what Mama always said about herself.

"But what happened to the Sat— To the molasses?" Charlotte asked. She had almost said "the Saturday father" but caught herself just in time.

"There isna any," Mama said. "I fear we'll have no more until the blockade is lifted; not even Bacon's store can get it right now. I'm sorry, Lew," she said to Papa. "We'll have to eat our pudding without it."

Cornmeal pudding with molasses was Papa's very favorite of all the new foods he had learned to eat since he had come to America fifteen years ago. He had never eaten molasses in Scotland, where he and Mama had grown up.

Papa shrugged. "We canna expect to go withoot makin' some sacrifices noo and then, when there's a war on," he said.

Always the war. War meant fighting, Charlotte knew, but what did that have to do with molasses?

"What's a blockade?" Tom asked.

Lewis spoke up quickly. "It's when someone blocks a harbor so no ships can get in or out. Those blasted British have got Boston Harbor closed so tight, you couldn't get a rowboat through, let alone a merchant ship."

"Lewis!" Mama said sternly, and Papa raised his eyebrows.

"Beg pardon," Lewis mumbled. "But I'd like to know what I *should* call 'em. They're our enemies, after all."

"Still, that be no excuse for rough language," Papa said.

And Mama demanded, "Have you ivver heard your father usin' such a word?"

A funny look came over Lewis's face. "No, not *Papa* . . ." he said, letting the sentence trail off.

Mama stared at him a moment, and then

burst out laughing. "Meanin' you've heard *me* use it, I suppose. Och, my mother always said a day would come when my quick tongue would get me into trouble. And here it is, my own son tellin' me I'm a bad influence." She smiled a rueful smile. Mama's sharp tongue was as famous as her singing. She had a different song for every task. Mama said she had gotten the habit as a little girl in Scotland.

Well, if Mama had never had molasses as a little girl in Scotland, Charlotte knew she could do without molasses now. But this war was confusing! Until tonight, it had never had anything to do with her life, but now, it had taken all the molasses from Boston Harbor. *It* was the reason the poor father jug had to sit empty in the pantry. It was unsettling to think that something happening so far away could change things right here on her dinner table.

Charlotte hadn't even known molasses came from ships—she'd thought it came from the general store, or the stores in Boston. Suddenly the comfortable Saturday-night feeling was gone, and the world seemed very big outside the weathered brown door of the Tucker house.

Charlotte looked around the table. Why did no one else seem to mind? Lewis and Tom thought the war was exciting. Lydia didn't seem to care one way or the other, and Mary was not yet a year old. She didn't even know what molasses was, much less a war.

"Charlotte," Mama said after dinner, interrupting Charlotte's thoughts, "come and help me soak the salt cod for tomorrow."

Mama took the lid off the codfish barrel, and Charlotte lifted out five of the stiff, dried fish. She laid each one into the big pan of water Lydia had filled. The fish would soak all night, and by tomorrow morning they would be soft enough to cook. Salt cod was Sunday's special dinner, just as baked beans and corn pudding belonged to Saturday night. Preparing the cod with Mama was one of the very best parts of Saturday night. She sang Charlotte a funny song and the war began to feel far away again.

But it was hard to stop thinking about all the things that were happening. Until now, Charlotte had not thought of the world as something that spread far beyond the places she'd been. There was her own house on Tide Mill Lane. There was Papa's blacksmith shop across the way, and Washington Street that ran in front of it. There were the other things on that street: the gristmill, the potter's shop, other houses, and down the road the meeting-house and Roxbury Common. If you kept following the road, Charlotte knew, you would get to the city of Boston. Boston seemed to be a kind of grown-up Roxbury, with even more houses and shops and mills. If you needed something that couldn't be found in Roxbury, you went to Boston to get it. But now you couldn't even get molasses in Boston, and Charlotte started to wonder where it came from. What else was out there, farther away than she'd ever imagined?

THE CORBIE AND THE CROW

W ill Payson was a tall young man from Dorchester who worked for Papa in the smithy. He was called a striker, because so much of his work was striking the hot iron with his hammer. He boarded with the Tuckers during the week and took nearly all his meals with them. Dorchester was not far, but it was too far for Will to go home to every night. He went home only for Saturday nights and Sundays, and always returned on Monday just as the sun was coming up.

Will was taller even than Papa, and his shoulders were thin, not broad like Papa's. He had laughing hazel eyes and an appealing way of furrowing his brow when he listened to someone speak. His hair was cut short, in the new fashion. He wore long, loose-fitting trousers called pantaloons instead of the tight, knee-length breeches Papa wore. Pantaloons had not been around very long, and mostly they were worn by young men.

Mama liked to tease Papa that he was not so very old; he ought to switch to pantaloons, too.

"Nay, I think not," Papa would say, shaking his head. "Breeches were good enough for me father, an' sure they be good enough for me."

Today, Charlotte was upstairs, buttoning up her dark blue homespun dress and tying on her gray muslin apron, when she and Lydia heard the low rumble of Will's voice. There was the lilting sound of Mama greeting him. Then footsteps, and Papa's soft voice. Then the *crash crash crash* of Lewis going down the stairs two at a time, and the *thump thump thump* of heavy-footed Tom following him.

Charlotte and Lydia were usually the last

ones to the kitchen in the mornings, for they had to do their upstairs work first. But on Mondays, when Will returned, Charlotte always had to fight not to rush through her chores. Today she was especially eager to see Will. She wanted to tell him about the missing molasses.

First, Charlotte had to help Lydia turn back the covers on their bed to let the sheets air out. She dusted the bedstead, the wooden chest beneath the window, and the little round table that held the washbasin and pitcher. Lydia swept the floor, singing all the while, for Lydia had Mama's way of singing as she worked. Then they had to do the same things in the room that Lewis and Tom shared with Will.

When at last they arrived in the kitchen, no one was there! Had Will already gone to work in the smithy? There was only a maze of footprints in the sand on the wooden floor. Mama kept the floorboards covered with a layer of sand, to catch grease and spills. Every night she swept that sand into a pretty pattern of curves and swirls.

Just as Charlotte was starting to wonder where everyone was, Mama came in carrying a pail full to the brim with milk.

"Ah, there you are, Lottie," said Mama cheerily, crossing to the pantry and pouring the milk into two wide, shallow pans. "I need you to run down to the root cellar and bring me four good big potatoes for breakfast."

So Charlotte ran through the lean-to and around the house to the outer cellar door. The air was chill and the sky was still pink at the edges. The unpainted clapboard walls of the house looked gray in the morning light. Mama said they ought to have the house painted one of these years but there was always so much other work to do that no one had time. It was an old house, older even than Mama and Papa, and it was not as smart as the new houses that were appearing all over Roxbury. But it was sturdy and snug, and Mama said it suited them fine.

Charlotte went around to the back of the house. She saw Papa and Lewis out in the barnyard forking hay into a pile for the cows,

Patience and Mollie, and their two knobby-legged calves. In the shady corners of the yard were a few last clumps of snow, and Charlotte shivered. She didn't know how Lewis could stand to walk on the cold, damp ground in his bare feet. She saw Tom filling the wood box, and Will walking toward the smithy.

She hurried down the cellar steps to the big wooden potato bin. A pale rectangle of light fell upon the earthen floor from the open door at the top of the stairs. Charlotte dug down into the sand and counted out potatoes, two, three, four. They felt cool and firm.

Back in the kitchen, Mama quickly peeled the potatoes and put them in a skillet to fry. Lydia came in from the parlor and handed Mary to Charlotte. The baby's long skirt trailed from Charlotte's lap and reached halfway to the floor.

"Don't let her muss her gown," Lydia told Charlotte. "Today she's wearing lavender silk with ribbons of purest gold."

Of course Mary wasn't really wearing silk. Lydia was only pretending. It would be silly to put real silk and ribbons on the baby—it was hard enough just keeping Mary's plain muslin frock clean.

Lydia went out to feed the chickens, while Charlotte held a squirming Mary upon her lap and watched Mama make the bread dough.

She gathered ingredients from a shelf above the hearth lined with all sorts of wonderful objects. Charlotte knew what every one of them was for: the prickly tin nutmeg grater, the potato masher, the shiny tin measuring cups lined up like a row of ducks. She liked the spidery black script on the labels of the spice jars. Each word meant a different smell: *curry, cinnamon, cayenne*. Charlotte could not read the names, but she knew the smells by heart.

Beside the fireplace was a brick bake oven. It was a large square hole built into the wall, with bricks making its top and bottom and sides. The hole was closed off by a metal door. When Mama wanted to bake something, she took off the door and built a fire inside, right on the bricks.

Mama was going to bake today. Even if

Monday hadn't always been baking day, Charlotte would have known by the fire blazing hot and orange in the brick oven.

First Mama took out the wooden flour box with the yeast sponge inside. The sponge was a mixture of yeast, cornmeal, rye flour, and water. Mama had mixed it last night. While Charlotte watched, Mama kneaded flour into the sponge until she had a thick dough. Then she lifted the big lump of dough out of the box and put it on the table to finish kneading.

At last it was ready to rise. Mama put the dough in a bowl, covered it with a cloth, and left it to sit a while.

"Go and sweep the parlor, Charlotte," Mama said. "Take Mary with you."

Charlotte didn't like to sweep when the baby was there. Mary clung to her legs and grabbed at her apron, or she sat down right in the middle of the dust pile.

But at last the floor was swept and breakfast was ready. The smell of fried potatoes came out of the kitchen ahead of Mama. There were eggs, too, and cold slices of beef and fried cornmeal pudding. Papa and the boys came in, and Will hurried in from the smithy.

It was exciting to all be together again after a long weekend without Will; but at first, everyone was too busy eating to talk. Even Charlotte was so hungry that she ate two slices of pudding. The pudding made her remember, with some sorrow, the empty molasses jug.

"Will," she said. "Did you know that there's no more molasses?"

"Yes, Miss Charlotte," he said evenly. "That's the war for you."

Charlotte liked to talk to Will, for he listened just as carefully to small girls as he did to mothers and fathers. He never laughed when someone asked a question, even if everyone else in the room did.

But now even Will was talking about war, when usually he talked of a great many interesting things. Birds, for example—he knew everything there was to know about them. He could tell the name of a bird just by looking at its nest or listening to its song. When he whistled, he sounded so much like a real bird that Charlotte half expected to see one perched on his head.

Once, last month, Charlotte and Tom had come upon Will standing among the trees behind the smithy, watching a small brown bird hop among the old leaves on the ground. The bird had a white chest and red patches on its sides, and Will said she was called a towhee, after her song. He whistled to her, softly, "To-whee! To-whee!" and the bird cocked her head and answered. Her fluty call seemed to say *Drink-your-TEA! Drink-your-TEA!* Tom and Charlotte burst out laughing, for it *was* nearly teatime, and Will often got so absorbed in watching birds that he was late to the table. Their laughter startled the bird, and she flew away. But Will said she would come back, for she was nesting; he showed them the small nest half hidden in the brush, with five tiny speckled eggs inside.

Charlotte liked Will so much that, for a while, she had had a secret plan for Lydia to marry him as soon as she was old enough. That way, Will would always stay with the family.

But this morning, as they were clearing the breakfast table, Will was telling Mama that he was going to marry a girl named Lucy. She lived in Dorchester, not far from his father's farm, Will explained. Just as soon as he had saved enough money for a house, he was going to bring Lucy to Roxbury to live.

"You'll like her, Mrs. Tucker," he told Mama. "She's a lot like you—does her churning on Monday."

Charlotte was confused. "But we churn on Thursdays," she said.

Mama laughed. "That's just Will's way o' sayin' that his Lucy has ideas of her own," she said. "Doesna do what the neighbors do just because it's always been done that way."

"Oh," Charlotte said. Here was something else to think about. Why *shouldn't* you churn your butter on Thursdays? Everyone she knew did. Recently it seemed to Charlotte that strange new ideas met her at every turn. Just when you thought you understood a thing, something new came along for you to figure out.

So she was not going to have Will for a

brother after all. At least he wasn't going to move away. He would bring Lucy to Roxbury, and maybe he would build his house nearby. That would be almost as nice as having Lydia marry Will. In fact, in some ways it might be even nicer—there was always the chance this Lucy was the sort of person who believed in giving doughnuts or taffy to little girls who came to visit. Charlotte hoped so.

By the time Charlotte and Lydia had washed and dried the breakfast dishes and Mama had rolled out two piecrusts, the fire in the brick oven had burned to coals. That meant the oven was hot enough to cook food now—too hot, in fact, for the bricks soaked up so much heat that Mama would have to let the oven cool down a little first, or her pies and bread would burn. She took the wooden ash shovel and scraped the hot embers out of the oven. Beside the oven hung a long-handled brush, and this Mama used to wipe away the last of the ashes. Then she hurried to her pie-crusts, and quickly put together two dried-apple pies, well sprinkled with cinnamon and brown sugar, with big lumps of butter beneath the strips of pastry on top.

Now it was time to check the oven to see if it had cooled enough to cook the pies. Mama had a special way to tell when it was cool enough. Charlotte had watched her so many times that she knew how to do it, too. She had never done it before, but today she thought she would help Mama. She stuck her arm into the oven and held it there very still.

"Mercy, lass!" Mama cried. But then she saw that Charlotte was being careful not to touch the oven walls.

Charlotte counted, "One, two, three . . ." She got as far as seven before her arm began to feel scorched. She pulled it out and waved it in the cool air. "Still too hot, Mama," she said.

"Aye, I'd say so," Mama said, staring at Charlotte. "Gracious, you gave me a turn."

"Yes, ma'am," Charlotte said. She did not see why Mama should be so surprised. She had only done what Mama did herself.

In a few minutes, Mama said Charlotte might check it again. This time Charlotte could keep her arm inside all the way to ten. That meant the oven was just the right temperature for pies. Mama slid the pies into place and closed the oven door. While the pies baked, she mixed up a cake to put in the oven after the bread. The brick oven took so much work and used so much wood, Mama did all her week's baking at once.

With the pie in the oven, Mama began to sing a song about a corbie and a crow. She explained that a corbie was a great black bird with a raspy kind of cry.

"The corbie wi' his roupy throat
Cried frae his leafless tree,
'Come o'er the loch, come o'er the loch,
Come o'er the loch wi' me.'
"The crow put up his sooty head
And cried, 'Where to? Where to?'
'To yonder field,' the corbie said,
'Where there is corn enoo.

"'The plowman plowed the land yestreen,
The farmer sowed this morn;

And we can make a full, fat meal
Frae off the broadcast corn.
And we can make a full, fat meal
Frae off the broadcast corn.'"

A sweet, spicy smell filled the kitchen as Mama sang. The pies were finished. Mama took them out and put the soft brown lump of bread dough into the oven.

"I'm going to ask Will to show me a corbie," Charlotte said once the bread was in the oven.

But Mama said she had never seen a corbie in America. They were Scottish birds. In that case, Charlotte would have to listen hard so she could at least sing Will the song about the corbie.

SPRING

Spring in Roxbury was a busy time for everyone. April faded into May in a green haze that crept over fields and treetops. The little purple crocuses that had poked through the snow were all gone now, and so was the snow. Robins hopped about in the brown garden and sunned themselves on the garden wall. Fragrant buds swelled and burst into bloom on the lilac bush beside the kitchen door.

The speckled eggs hatched in the towhee's nest. Will took Charlotte to see the five wide-mouthed nestlings peeping shrilly to their mother and her black-feathered husband. Charlotte could have stayed all day watching them, but Will said they would get on better if they were left to themselves. Whenever Charlotte went out, she listened for the mother's gentle voice reminding the world to *Drink-your-TEA, Drink-your-TEA.*

Every morning now, Lewis turned the six merino ewes out to graze in the meadow behind the garden. Their gray wool was long and curly, and soon it would be time for Papa to shear them. Then Mama would be busy for weeks, washing the fleeces and combing them smooth.

Spring was Papa's busiest season at the smithy. Farmers from miles around came to his shop for repairs and tools, and pots and pans, and door hinges and horseshoes and wagon parts. Anything with iron parts that needed fixing, Papa could fix. And if it couldn't be fixed, he could make a new one.

Sometimes Mama looked out the kitchen window at the smithy and shook her head. She said it was a wonder Papa ever got any work done at all, with the crowd of men and boys that was always hanging about over there. The farmers who brought in their tools, or their horses to be shod, liked to stay and talk for a while, exchanging news.

After dinner, when they were all sitting in the parlor, Mama scolded Papa about it. "You ought to send those fellows home to their farms," she said.

But Papa only smiled and said he liked to listen to the chatter while he worked.

"All the same," Mama teased, "they're no more than a bunch of gossips."

It wasn't gossip, Lewis said—it was important talk about the war. Lewis was very interested in the war news, and he had taken to reading the newspapers whenever he could get one. He spread the papers on the parlor table and shouted about the battles being fought far away on land and sea.

That night, there was news of a British fleet headed toward the American troops at Niagara.

"It says the British were expected to arrive by the fourth or fifth of May," Lewis cried.

"That's yesterday! Our boys could be whupping them right this minute and we wouldn't know it, it takes so long for news to get through."

He pounded the table with his hand, making Lydia jump. She had spread the contents of Mama's thread basket on the table in front of her and was sorting colors for her embroidery sampler.

"Lewis!" she complained.

"Easy, lad," Papa said from the corner where he sat playing checkers with Will.

"Yes, Papa," Lewis said, abashed. He sat back down at the table with the inky sheets spread out before him. Beside him, Tom leaned forward on his elbows to look at the drawings of ships and battle sites.

Mama sat in the big upholstered chair by the west window, where she could work without lighting a candle until the sun went down altogether. But the east side of the room was too dim for reading, so Mama let Lewis have a tallow candle on the dinner table. The burning candle filled the room with a smoky smell and made shadows dance upon the ceiling.

Charlotte sat on the floor at Mama's feet playing a game with a thimble and a button. The thimble was a house, the button a little man who lived there alone. Mary wanted to play, too, only she seemed to think both button and thimble looked like nice things to eat.

"Give it back, Mary," Charlotte said, trying for the hundredth time to pry open her sister's chubby fist.

Will scooped Mary up and rescued Charlotte's button. "Here you are, Lottie," he said. "I'll mind the baby for a while." Charlotte smiled at him gratefully. Will sat back down in his corner chair and gave Mary some of the wooden checkers he had captured from Papa.

"Go on, Lewis," Mama said. "What else does the paper have to say?"

Mama said half of what was written about the war was pure nonsense, but she made Lewis read the papers aloud, nonetheless. She sat bolt upright in her chair, knitting furiously and looking as if she might fly into the air if the news was against her liking.

Will liked to tease Mama by bringing home *The Yankee.* That was a newspaper that supported Mr. Madison and the war, and it outraged Mama.

Mr. Madison was the fourth President. There was no parade on his birthday, like there was for General George Washington, the first President of the United States. Will said perhaps there would be someday, when people came to see that he had done the right thing by declaring war on England.

"Surely you don't hold with the British navy boarding American ships and kidnapping our own sailors, Mrs. Tucker," he asked Mama. "Nor riling up the Indians against us and supplying them with arms."

"Of course not," Mama replied tartly. "But you know as well as I do that that business is only part of the story. Our government wants Canada, plain and simple. As if the President hasn't enough on his hands already, tryin' to keep America in one piece."

"Well, noo, we must be fair, Martha," Papa said. "Mr. Madison was no more eager to declare war on England than we are to be in it. Pushed into it, he was, by those land-hungry war hawks from the western territories."

"If I was President, I wouldna let meself be pushed into this war," said Mama.

Papa and Will exchanged a look. "I've nae doubt aboot that," Papa murmured.

"At any rate," said Will, "we're in it now, and we'd better win. My father nearly lost his life in the War for Independence. I'm an American, by gum, and I plan to remain one."

"I, too," said Papa in his quiet way.

Charlotte took the button man out of his house and walked him along a long narrow road made by the edge of a floorboard. He came to a table leg and, with great exertion, climbed it to peep over Lewis's arm at a tall-masted ship sailing on a flat white newspaper sea.

"Is that the molasses ship?" Charlotte asked. "The one that can't get through because of the clockade?"

Lewis guffawed. "It's *block*ade, you ninny."

Tom laughed, and worse, so did Lydia. It was infuriating; Lydia paid so little attention to the war that Charlotte doubted she even remembered why the molasses was gone.

"Easy, now," Mama chided. "I'll not have you mockin' each other."

"Beg pardon, Mama," Lewis said. "It's just so funny!"

Charlotte started to retort, but Will spoke up first. "As I recall, the ship in that drawing is a sloop of war, isn't she, Lewis? Your molasses ship would be a merchant vessel, Charlotte, from New Orleans or the West Indies."

"See, Lottie," said Lewis, not wanting to be left out, "here are the cannons. That's how you can tell she's a warship. This one is British. They've got her anchored off the coast of Connecticut, ready to attack one of our forts."

Attacks and blockades, ships and armies— lately the grown-ups and Lewis never seemed to talk about anything but the war. Tonight, Charlotte worried. What would happen if America lost the war? Suppose it meant there would never be any molasses again—ever? What if that was only the beginning of the things that changed?

Mama stood and held up her knitting to the window. "There, that's finished." It was a gray stocking for Papa. Its mate was already finished, and Mama took that one out of her workbasket and folded the two stockings together. A year ago, those stockings had been crinkly wool on the back of one of those merinos. Papa had sheared the fleece from the sheep's back, and Mama had washed it and combed it smooth with her spiky-toothed carding brushes. Then she had spun it into yarn on her spinning wheel. And now that yarn had been knitted into a pair of stockings.

Charlotte looked at these stockings, flat and soft and gray in Mama's hands. It seemed to her they were made of more than just wool. There was a whole year's worth of words and thoughts knitted into them like the tiny prickles of grass seed that sometimes stayed stuck in the wool even after it had been washed and carded and spun. All the words that had been spoken while

Mama's quick hands made the needles cross and uncross around the endless strand of wool were there, knitted into Papa's stockings.

Charlotte climbed into Mama's lap. Mama stroked her hair and cuddled her against her. Charlotte held the thimble tightly in her hand with the button man tucked inside it. The thimble was the button man's bed now, and it was time to go to sleep.

In the Garden

Planting time was passing. The beans and the peas were tucked into their rows. The squashes were planted, and the melons and radishes and turnips. Mama kept Lewis home from the smithy one day to get the potatoes into the ground. And every few days Mama checked the almanac to make sure the garden was coming along on schedule.

She sat in her armchair and turned the pages between their yellow covers. There was a pair of pages for each month of the year. The almanac told when to plant certain crops and when to harvest them. It said what the weather would be like, and when the moon would be full. It told when elections were to be held, and how to save your apple trees from caterpillars, and lots more things besides. There was a list of all the ships in the navy, which Lewis had read so many times that the almanac fell open to that page by itself.

Charlotte wished she could read it, too, but she could not read yet. Mama told her that the letters M-A-Y at the top of the page spelled the word *May*, and that was what month it was. On the left-hand page, Mama said, were the words *MAY hath 31 Days*. The right side said, *MAY, fifth Month*, and below that was a verse. Lydia especially liked that verse, and she asked Mama to read it so often that soon even Charlotte began to know it by heart.

It went:

> *The little wood songsters are*
> *tunefully singing,*

To hail the glad morning of each
    rising day;
And with their shrill echo, the vallies are
    ringing—
How sweet are their notes that descend
    from each spray.

Charlotte's birthday was in the next-to-last week of May. The almanac said to expect rain in plenty all that week and it was right. It kept right on raining on the morning of her birthday. Mama said that was a lucky thing, for if it had been fine, they'd have had to work all day in the garden. Instead, after dinner, Mama put Mary in bed for a nap and called Lydia and Charlotte into the cozy corner beside the kitchen hearth. She said Charlotte was six now, and that was old enough to sew doll clothes.

"But I don't have a doll," Charlotte said. Her heart thumped a little because it was her birthday.

"Aye, I suppose that's so—for the moment," Mama said, glancing at Lydia. Lydia giggled, her eyes shining with a secret.

Mama reached into her apron pocket and brought out a clothespin. Charlotte felt a rush of disappointment, but then she saw that Mama had painted a face on the round knob at the top of the clothespin. The doll had round black eyes and a smiling red mouth, and glossy wings of painted black hair parted in the middle. She had little arched eyebrows and red dots for cheeks.

The rest of her was just wooden clothespin. Mama said it was up to Charlotte to dress her, and to think of a name. There were so many names to choose from, Charlotte could not decide. But Mama said naming was a grave matter, and it was wise to think on it awhile.

Lydia was still eager with more of the secret. "What about the dress, Mama?" she asked.

Mama's hand went to her apron pocket again. "I've cut a bit o' cloth for you," she told Charlotte. "'Tis up to you to turn it into a frock."

Mama's hand opened and showed Charlotte a square of fabric. Charlotte squealed in surprise, and Lydia clapped her hands.

"It was my idea," she said.

Mama laughed. "Aye, you've got your sister to thank for this. I'd forgotten I had it tucked away."

The cloth was a piece of a gown Mama had worn long ago. It was a lovely plaid with dark blue and pale blue stripes crossing one another. It came from Scotland, where Mama had grown up. She said all the girls in her county had worn blue-plaid gowns and petticoats like this. Now Charlotte's doll could look just the way Mama had as a girl.

Lydia showed Charlotte how to bend a piece of wire around the clothespin for arms, while Mama cut a dress pattern out of brown paper. She helped Charlotte trace the pattern onto the pretty cloth, and then she cut it out. Charlotte already knew how to sew a nice straight hem; Mama had made her practice on a sheet all winter long. Charlotte hadn't enjoyed it. But now, Mama said, Charlotte would learn the fun of sewing.

"I hated sewing until I made my first frock for one o' my bairns," Mama explained. "There's naught sweeter than puttin' tiny wee stitches into a gown for your own wee babe. You'll see, now you have a bairn o' your own."

But the next day was sunny. Mama threw open all the doors in the morning, to air out the house. The little wood songsters made a cheery noise among the apple blossoms in the side yard. The air smelled sweet. It was a good day to plant.

Mama spread a piece of canvas sacking on the ground beside the garden wall and put Mary on it. The long trailing skirt of Mary's baby frock fanned out next to her, and Mama pinned it down with a stone so that Mary couldn't crawl away.

The vegetables were all planted now, so it was time to plant herbs between the rows. Mama brought out the seeds she had saved from last fall, little specks of black and brown in small brown-paper envelopes sealed with flour paste. Those specks did not look anything like the plants they would become, but Mama knew exactly which speck would turn into which herb, and how deep to plant it.

Mama knew everything there was to know about herbs. All summer, she collected them and hung them to dry in upside-down bunches from the lean-to's rafters. Sage and lavender and rosemary, pennyroyal and thyme and hyssop. Bee balm, betony, candytuft—the names were like a song. Mama knew just which ones to add to soup or stuffing to make it tastier, and which ones to flavor cakes with. She could brew them into teas that cured illness or helped you to sleep. She dried them and sewed the crumbly leaves inside little cloth pillows that she sold to Mr. Bacon's store, or traded to the neighbors. Those pillows smelled lovely, and if you put one between your sheets, it kept bedbugs away. It seemed there was nothing you couldn't do with the right combination of herbs, if you just knew how.

Mama poured a packet of lovage seeds into Charlotte's palm. Then, taking up her hoe, Mama went along the rows making holes for the seeds. Charlotte tucked one or two seeds into each hole, and Lydia came behind, covering them with earth.

"What is lovage for?" Charlotte asked.

Mama said lovage leaves tasted delicious in salads and soups. They soothed bee stings, too, she said, and they could be boiled in water to make medicine for the eyes and throat. "Some folks even take the root and candy it in a sugar syrup," she said, "though I've never tried that meself."

"How do you know all that, Mama?"

"I learned it when I was a lass," Mama said, "from an old woman who lived away out on the moor at the edge of me father's land."

"But how did she know?" Charlotte asked.

"I suppose she learned from her mother, or her mother's mother."

"But how did *they* know?" Charlotte persisted. "Who figured it out first?"

"Ah, we'd a story about that when I was young," Mama said. "'Twas about a great hero who was killed in a battle. It's said that when he died, herbs sprang up in the grass where his body fell, each one holdin' a fragment of his strength. Beneath his stout heart that never knew fear, there grew a lily of the valley.

To this day, its root holds the power to stimulate the heart. Where his head lay came a wee green herb that could cure headaches and wounds of the head. Betony, it was. And another, a tall spike of purple flowers with dark spots in their throats, that had been crushed beneath the warrior's middle—people found it made a good strong medicine to make you bring up something that's ailin' your stomach."

"Foxglove!" Charlotte cried. Mama had made a medicine out of foxglove for the miller's wife last winter. It came up by itself every year over by the garden wall.

"Aye," Mama said, pleased. "Fairy glove, we called it in Scotland. And that puts me in mind of another tale me mother used to tell."

MAMA'S STORY OF THE FAIRY'S NURSEMAID

One evening as a young woman named Meggie sat by her fire singin' to her bairn, a beautiful lady came into her cottage, dressed in a fairy mantle. The fairy lady carried a bairn that cried and fussed in her arms.

"What shall ye do for my child?" asked the lady. Meggie hardly knew what to say, but the squallin' of the fairy's bairn went straight to her heart, and she said, "Give me the child to nurse."

"Do that, and he'll nivver want," said the pretty lady, and quick as lightning, she was gone.

Meggie nursed the fairy's bairn right alongside her own bonny son. The poor hungry bairn stopped its terrible wailin', and when it had taken its fill, it fell fast asleep wi' a little smile on its wee ugly face—for as everyone knows, an uglier thing than a fairy's bairn there isn't in all the world.

The next morning, to her great surprise, she found two little suits of clothes laid out on the table, just the sizes to fit the fairy's bairn and her own bonny son. And a loaf of fine bread there was—fairy bread, that tastes of honey and fills you with more vigor than meat.

Every week after that a fairy loaf appeared on Meggie's table, and plenty o' fine clothes to keep the two bairns snug all the winter through. Sure and Meggie did treat the two of them just the same, and a kinder mother there never was.

On a midsummer afternoon the fairy lady came back. She looked at her bairn and was pleased to see what a fine, healthy child it had grown into. It clapped its little hands wi' joy to see its mother. The lady took the child into her arms and thanked Meggie for tendin' it so well.

"Follow me now," said the lady. They walked out of the house and through the barley field, and they kept on goin' until they came to a silvery wood on a green hill. At the far edge of the wood, where the sun shone on the slope, a door opened in the green grass of the hillside.

The fairy stooped and plucked a spike of foxglove. She dabbed a few drops of a sparkling nectar onto Meggie's left eyelid. Then Meggie followed the lady through the green door into a land lovelier than anything she had ever seen or imagined. All green and golden and blue, it was, with clear streams and rich fields and trees laden with fruit. At the foot of the tallest tree was a chest filled with webs of fine cloth, and salves and ointments to cure any ill, and more of those honey-sweet loaves Meggie had eaten all the winter through.

"For you," said the fairy lady, "and a mount to carry it home." Up trotted a beautiful snow-white pony led by a little crooked gnome, who lifted the chest onto the pony's back and bid it to follow her home.

Then the lady breathed gently on Meggie's eye, and just like that, all of it was gone. Meggie found herself back at the edge of the silver wood, her little son held tight in her arms and the white pony nibblin' at the grass with the chest o' treasures on its back.

But Meggie happened to catch sight o' the foxglove spike the fairy had plucked. Sure enough, there was the tiniest wee bit of magic dew left, and this did Meggie dab onto her eyelids just as the fairy lady had done.

Then Meggie went home with all the treasures the lady had given her. A long and happy life she had, and always she had the gift of seeing sprites and fairies that were hidden from other mortals. One day many years later she happened to spy the beautiful fairy lady whose child she had nursed. Meggie ran to the lady and took her hand, asking how the fairy child was and sayin' she hoped it had grown up as well and hearty as her own son had.

The fairy gasped and stared at Meggie.

"What eye do ye see me with?" she asked.

"Why, with them both," answered Meggie, and with that the fairy leaned forward and breathed on Meggie's eyes. And from that day forth Meggie could see fairies no more.

"But she got off lucky," Mama added, "for the fairy lady might have taken away *all* Meggie's eyesight and left her blind."

If Charlotte had been Meggie, she thought, she'd have done just the same thing.

THE ROAD TO SCOTLAND

One day, after planting time had passed and before weeding time had come around, Mama went to Mr. Bacon's store. There she bought a piece of creamy white muslin, which she said was to be a new school apron for Charlotte. Charlotte was surprised to hear it was almost time to go to school.

Charlotte was not sure she wanted to go to school, especially when Lydia and Lewis didn't have to go. The big boys and girls went only in the winter. Papa needed Lewis in the shop and in the hayfield, and Mama must have

Lydia's help around the house and garden. Mostly Lydia watched Mary so Mama could work.

Just now there was so much going on at home, Charlotte hated to miss it. She would miss the vegetables getting ripe in the garden and, later on, the picking and the canning and the pickling.

"Who will sweep the hearth while I'm at school, Mama?" she asked.

Mama touched Charlotte's cheek and said, "Lydia will do it. School's naught but three months, Charlotte. You must get every bit of it that you can."

Lydia, who was rocking Mary in the corner, made a face. She would rather go to school to see her friends than stay home and mind the baby.

Charlotte wandered out to the garden. The beans were getting tall, their long curling vines climbing the wooden stakes Mama had pushed into the ground. The newly planted herbs were beginning to sprout. Tiny green spikes peeked out of the soil.

Charlotte thought about all the things that Mama knew about the garden. She hadn't learned them in school; she'd learned them back in Scotland. Maybe Charlotte didn't have to go to school after all. It took no more than a second for Charlotte to make up her mind. She must go to Scotland.

Mama and Papa had come from Scotland to Boston—first Papa, and then, a few months later, Mama had joined him. They had come together from Boston to Roxbury. Charlotte knew just how to get to Boston, and she supposed once she got there, she could ask for directions to Scotland. Mama said Scotland was across the sea, which was evidently a big water like the brook that cut through Roxbury, perhaps a little bigger. There was a bridge across Stony Brook, and Charlotte felt certain there would be a bridge across the sea to Scotland, too.

But the first thing to do was to get to Boston. When Papa went to Boston, he usually borrowed a wagon, to carry things home in. But Mama made the trip on foot sometimes, to do shopping. Even Lydia had been there, once or twice.

Charlotte tried to remember what Lydia had said. If you walked along Washington Street right through the center of town and beyond, you came to the Neck. The Neck was the part of Washington Street that connected Roxbury to Boston. Lydia had told Charlotte all about how the road there crossed over a shallow bay.

Charlotte was pretty sure that a bay was another kind of water like Stony Brook or the sea. That meant she would cross over three big waters to get to Scotland: first Stony Brook, and then the bay, and then the sea.

It did not sound so hard. Charlotte went into the kitchen to switch her everyday bonnet for her good Sunday one. Mama always wore her best bonnet when she went to Boston.

The chicken Mama was roasting was beginning to smell good. Charlotte would have to walk very fast if she was going to be back in time for dinner. But thinking of dinner and smelling the chicken made her feel very hungry *now*. Very quietly she took the tin from the cupboard and put some sugar cookies into her apron pocket alongside her clothespin doll. The doll's pretty dress was finished, but she still did not have a name. Charlotte stood on tiptoe to reach her Sunday bonnet on its peg by the door. She tied its red laces all by herself and slipped out of the house.

She crossed Tide Mill Lane and cut between the trees behind the smithy, coming out onto Washington Street just across from the gristmill. The mill's big wooden wheel turned around in the swift waters of Stony Brook, and the millpond lay flat and gray beyond it. Charlotte crossed Stony Brook on the bridge and followed the road toward the center of town.

The road was busy with carts, some pulled by horses and some by oxen. The drivers touched their hats and nodded at Charlotte, and Charlotte remembered to curtsy each time. The proud, gleaming horses made a brisk *clop-clop* sound, and the burly oxen made a heavy *clump-clump, clump-clump*. Their hooves left dents in the soft dirt of the road.

Walking to Boston took a long time. Charlotte ate one cookie, and then she ate two more. That left three cookies, and she supposed she had better save them for the walk home. Charlotte hoped it would not take long to reach Scotland, once she got to Boston. Surely it was getting close to dinnertime now. Without thinking about it, she nibbled on another cookie. A yellow dog trotted out of a lane and fell into step beside her. It looked up at her with friendly eyes and an open mouth, as if to say, *Good day, miss. I could use a nibble, too*. Charlotte sighed and broke off a bit of cookie for it. It was not polite to eat in front of others without sharing, even dogs.

She came to the wide, shop-lined square that was the town common, where the meeting-house was and the new town hall. After that, she passed a lot of shops and houses, and several streets that ran into Washington Street. She had not known Washington Street was so long. Through her bonnet, the sun felt hot on the top of her head.

"I'm going to Boston," she told the yellow

dog. The dog gave a cheerful bark then turned off down a lane.

"Oh!" Charlotte said. "Good-bye, then." Without the dog, she felt a little lonely. There were many people about, ladies in their ribboned bonnets with baskets over their arms, farmers in tall straw hats and homespun shirts, young men in pantaloons laughing in doorways. But none of them paid Charlotte any mind, and that made her feel even lonelier.

She put her hand in her apron pocket and squeezed her clothespin doll. Charlotte had been thinking very hard about a name since her birthday, but she had not decided on one yet. Mama said choosing a name was like choosing a good boughten cloth: you must choose something that would wear well and fit the wearer, for it must last a long time.

Charlotte thought about all the names she knew. Mama's name was Martha. Will's sweetheart was named Lucy. Mr. Stowe, the cooper, had three daughters named Anne, Jane, and Hannah. They were all very pretty names, but none of them seemed right for the little rosy-cheeked doll in her blue-plaid dress.

All the time she was thinking about this, Charlotte was looking for the Neck. Lydia had said there was water on both sides of the road, like crossing a bridge. Seagulls squawked over-head—that meant water was nearby. But Charlotte walked and walked and did not see a big water.

She came to a marshy place where there were no houses or shops. On both sides of the road, the wet ground was studded with clumps of stringy grass and tall, velvety stands of cat-tails pointing stubbornly at the sky. There was a damp, salty smell to the air. There were small pools and rivulets of water in places, but the road did not cross over these, and so this could not be the Neck.

Far ahead, Charlotte could see some houses spread out upon a hill. She had not known there were so many houses in Roxbury. She watched the houses come closer and closer as she walked.

A coach came toward her, pulled by two great horses. The driver tipped his hat to

Charlotte as he went by. She wanted to ask him how far it was to Boston, but she was feeling shy. As the coach went past, she caught a glimpse of a little boy with curled yellow hair looking through the window. Charlotte wished she could ride in a coach like that all the way to Scotland. She was getting very tired.

Then a cart came toward her, pulled by two placid oxen. The cart was loaded high with sacks and packages, and a man walked beside it. The man wore a stained leather apron and a worn flannel cap. It looked just like Papa's cap and apron, and when the man got closer, he looked at Charlotte in surprise. It *was* Papa.

"Charlotte, lass!" Papa cried. "Whatever are ye doin' here, child?" He stopped the oxen.

Charlotte did not say anything. She was surprised to see him; she had had no idea that Papa had gone to Boston this morning. The thought came to her all of a sudden that perhaps Papa and Mama would not be pleased she had come so far by herself. But she was very glad to see Papa all the same.

Papa's blue eyes were full of questions. "Do

ye ken where ye are, lass? Ye're not a stone's throw from Boston! This is no place for a wee lass on her own," Papa's voice was grave. He squatted down and squeezed Charlotte's shoulders. "Where did ye think ye was goin', child?"

"To Scotland, Papa," said Charlotte. She explained about Mama and the garden and school, and how she was going to Boston to look for the bridge that would take her over the sea to Scotland.

Papa's slow smile spread across his face. "Ah, lass," he said, "ye'll no make it tae Scotland this day, I fear. 'Tis a sight farther than you realize. Your mama and I, we sailed on ships to come to this country. Three months on board, I was, and your mither's journey was nearly half a year!"

Charlotte's heart fell. Her eyes felt like crying, and her throat felt too tight to talk. Nothing was as she had expected it to be. Now it was as if there was even more she didn't know.

"Dinna cry," Papa said. Charlotte *did* cry then. Between sobs she choked out a question.

"What's the sea, Papa? I thought it was a big water like Stony Brook."

"Like Stony—" Papa raised his eyes heavenward and whistled. "Have ye really lived your whole life a mile frae the sea withoot knowin' what it is? 'Tis a great wide stretch o' water, bigger than anything ye can imagine. Look, there—" he said, pointing eastward across the flats. "That's South Boston Bay, across there. A bay is a place where the sea cozies up tae the land. When the tide is in, the bay fills up all this place wi' seawater."

"Oh!" Charlotte said. She felt very much surprised. "Is this the Neck, Papa?"

"Aye," Papa said. "And those are the streets of Boston just ahead of ye, there. Ye came a great way on your own." His eyes were solemn now, and a little stern. "Ye're a plucky lass, Lottie, but ye're not to come this way again, mind. The Neck is no place for a girl your age on her own."

"Yes, Papa," she whispered. She could not help but stare at the houses she had seen scattered on the hillside in front of her. She had been looking right at Boston and had not known it.

Papa lifted Charlotte in his arms and carried her to the oxcart. "I can walk, Papa," Charlotte said, so Papa put her down, and she walked alongside him as he guided the oxen toward home. It was Mr. Waitt's oxcart and oxen; Papa had borrowed them in exchange for repairing the ox chains and the axle.

Every few steps, Charlotte looked back over her shoulder and saw the houses of Boston grow smaller. She felt silly, now, to think that she had thought she could make it all the way to Scotland and back before dinner. But it was not her fault no one had told her how big the sea was.

GREAT HILL

Back at home, Mama scolded Charlotte and said she must never go near the Neck alone. "You might wander off in the flats and lose yourself," Mama said. "I should hate to think what would happen if you got caught out in the marshes wi' the tide comin' in."

"Yes, ma'am," Charlotte said. She felt disappointed; she would have liked to go back at high tide and see the sea licking at the fence posts. But she knew Mama meant what she said, and so she promised to stay away from the Neck and the salt marsh. It meant that she would have to go to school, but Charlotte guessed that would be all right.

Mama told Charlotte to wash up and hurry to the table. The chicken was sliced and on the table already. A warm smell of fried potatoes hung in the air, and steam rose from a bowl of mashed squash. There was a dish of pickled cauliflower and another filled with a golden quivering mass of pumpkin preserves made last fall. Mama said Charlotte must wipe all the dishes after dinner and put them away herself for a whole week, as punishment.

"Aye, that's just," Papa said, nodding gravely. "You stay close by your mither this afternoon and be a good lass. But when the clock strikes four, come to the smithy." He would not say what for. Charlotte wondered about it all through dinner, and she wondered even harder as she wiped the dishes afterward and put them in the cupboard. It was not likely to be something nice waiting for her in the smithy after what she'd done this morning, but she didn't think it could be anything too bad, either. Papa and Mama did not seem angry, only stern, and they had already given her a punishment.

At last it was four o'clock. Lydia walked with her to the smithy, holding Charlotte's hand. She said it was to keep her company, but Charlotte suspected Lydia only wanted to know what the surprise was.

Charlotte stepped out of the bright sun into the cool, dim shop. Papa smiled when he saw her.

"Well, lads," Papa said to Will and Lewis and Tom, "I want ye tae come along, too. We'll close the shop airly, this once."

Charlotte and Lydia looked at each other. This was exciting. Papa led them across the lane to the house. Mama was out in the garden with Mary, and Papa called to her. "Everyone must come," he said.

Mama's eyes lit up, and she snatched off her apron. She loved surprises. She lifted Mary to her hip and ran to catch up. Charlotte laughed to see Mama running like a little girl.

Papa led the way down the lane toward Washington Street. As they drew near the wide road, Mama slowed down and straightened her skirts. Her cheeks were flushed, and her blue eyes danced. She grinned at Papa.

"You might have given me some warning," she scolded. "Me wi' me oldest dress on and no bonnet!"

"We're not going anywhere sae fancy," Papa said, with a twinkle in his eye. He strode calmly across Washington Street, lifting his hat to a lady and gentleman riding past in a large-wheeled buggy. The lady's eyes widened at the sight of Papa's sooty face and hands, and the even sootier faces and hands of Will and the boys, and Mama with nothing on her head but her plain linen cap. The lady's mouth pursed up in an "In-*deed*!" kind of way, and Mama laughed again.

"I canna blame her," she said as the buggy rolled past. "Never in me life have I seen such a raggle-taggle crew as we are today!"

Charlotte hurried to keep up with Papa. Lewis ran ahead so he could be first to get where they were going, but he didn't know where that was, and so he had to keep looking back over his shoulder to make sure everyone was still behind him.

"That way," Papa told him, pointing, and they followed a path that took them to Great Hill. That was a big hill that rose behind Mr. Ebenezer Craft's farm. Charlotte had seen Great Hill every day of her life, but she had never climbed it. Papa said she would climb it now.

Houses dotted the hillside, and higher up a rail fence cut across it like a collar. A great black crow sat surveying the world in the top of an oak tree.

"Why, look, Charlotte," Will said, "there's the corbie's friend, come to see how the pickings are in America." For Charlotte had told him all about the corbie and the crow from Mama's song.

"Why aren't there any corbies in America?" she asked.

"Well, I suppose birds are like people. There's some kinds of birds that never leave the place where they were born. And there's others that travel the world, looking for the best spot to build their nest."

"Like Mama and Papa!"

"That's right."

They had come to the top of the hill. Papa said, "Now turn aroond and look. There's where you were today, Lottie."

Charlotte looked down at the bumpy tops of trees and the stark angles of rooftops. Beyond them was spread a vast field of blue. A dark line cut across the blue, and Papa said that was the Neck. The tide had come in, and seawater had filled in all that marshy space she had seen this morning. The road was the only dry place left. It was strange to think she had been on that very road today.

On the other side of the watery blue field were small dots and smudges that Papa said were the buildings of Boston. They speckled a round slope that was the same hill Charlotte had seen from the road. Papa pointed to a glint of gold against the pale blue sky. That was the dome of the State House, he said, which the famous Mr. Paul Revere and his brother had covered with copper. So that was Boston.

Then Papa pointed to the east. Away out there, the blue of the water melted into the blue of the sky. You could not tell where the water ended. Papa said it practically did not end; it stretched on and on for more miles than Charlotte could imagine. He pointed to a black speck in the blue and said that was a ship, a British frigate probably, part of the blockade.

Mama put Mary down to crawl in the grass. Lydia sat down beside her and began picking small white-petaled oxeyes for a daisy chain. Tom and Lewis began a game of ships and ran about pretending to fire their cannons upon each other.

But Charlotte only stood there staring at the glittering blue edge of the sea. That edge was the beginning of a water as big as half a year. Far, far on the other side was Scotland, the green country where Mama and Papa had lived. Charlotte was happy that they were all together in America. In Roxbury, at home.

ON SCHOOL STREET

On the first Monday in June, Charlotte put on her blue linen dress and the new white muslin apron. It was her first day of school and she was nervous.

The dress had gotten too short, so Mama had added a ruffle to the bottom. Charlotte liked to look down and see the crisp edge of her apron and the ruffle sticking out beneath. The apron had two pockets. Into the left one, Charlotte put her clothespin doll. Tomorrow, she promised the apron, she would put the doll on the other side. Neither pocket must be made to feel left out.

"And I must think of a name for you, poor thing," she told the doll.

Mama had made Tom, who had been to summer school last year, put on his new blue shirt with the buttons on the bottom that fastened onto his pantaloons. The buttons curved over Tom's round stomach in a wide half circle that was exactly like the frown on his face. Tom hated wearing his button-up pantaloons.

"Not the jacket, too!" he begged, but Mama was firm. Gloomily he pulled on the jacket.

He was somewhat consoled, however, by the special breakfast Mama had made, of boiled beef and eggs. Afterward Mama gave Tom their dinner basket packed with bread and cheese and some ginger cookies, all wrapped in a red-and-white-checked napkin. Charlotte longed to carry the basket. But Mama said Tom must carry it to school, and Charlotte could carry it home.

Charlotte had her own schoolbook to carry to school, though. It was scuffed and worn, for Tom had used it, and Lydia, and Lewis. It had a yellow cover with the letters P-R-I-M-E-R on it in black. Mama told her they spelled *primer*, and that a primer was a book for learning to read.

Charlotte felt proud to have her own schoolbook, even if it was a little old.

Tom had his book, too, a slim brown one that had water spots on the cover, from a puddle that Lewis had splashed in when he was only seven, the age Tom was now. Tom threw the book into the basket on top of the napkin.

"The cookies!" Charlotte cried. "You'll break them to bits."

But Tom only shrugged and said, "Won't make them taste any different."

"They will," Charlotte insisted. Tom just stuck out his tongue, and Charlotte sighed.

"You're older than me," she said. "You ought to have more sense."

She followed him along Washington Street to Stony Brook. They passed Mr. Waitt's gristmill, where, through the open door, they could see the heavy millstones turning and turning, grinding a stream of grain into flour.

Tom liked the mill almost as much as he liked Papa's smithy. Forgetting to be grumpy about his jacket and his buttons, he swung the dinner basket around in the air like the mill wheel. Charlotte felt nearly frantic thinking about the cookies.

They turned onto Centre Street, a broad, rutted road that skirted Stony Brook. Wood lilies blazed orange-red at the roadside.

They went around a curve in the road, and there, just ahead of them, Charlotte got her first glimpse of their teacher, Miss Heath. Charlotte knew Miss Heath well; she was their neighbor. The windows of their house looked out on Miss Heath's father's land.

As far back as Charlotte could remember, Miss Heath had come calling with her mother, Mrs. John Heath, to spend snowy afternoons sewing in Mama's cozy parlor. But Miss Heath had been just Amelia then.

Now she was a grown-up lady of seventeen who wore her hair piled on top of her head. Charlotte must remember to call her "Miss Heath."

Miss Heath taught school only in the summers. The winter term was taught by a schoolmaster who came down from Boston. Charlotte had heard frightening stories about how he whipped children or made them stand in the freezing corner farthest from the fireplace when they did not know their lessons. She was very glad to have her nice neighbor, Miss Heath, as her first teacher.

Charlotte said good day and made a curtsy. It was a very good curtsy, and she felt quite proud. Amelia—Miss Heath—would see that Charlotte had grown up a great deal, now that she was five years old and ready for school. Tom bowed solemnly, staring at the teacher with his round eyes. He was always bashful around ladies. Charlotte thought with some satisfaction that now he would not be able to swing the dinner basket around.

Miss Heath smiled at them and said good day. She wore a green bonnet trimmed with ribbons and flowers, and over her ruffled muslin gown, she' wore a short, lacy jacket called a spencer. She was pretty and plump, with tendrils of black hair peeping out from under her bonnet.

"Shall we walk together?" she asked. She held out her hand for Charlotte to hold. Charlotte was suddenly glad she did not have to carry the basket. She was so proud to be walking to school with her new teacher that she quite forgot she had not wanted to go to school this summer.

The district schoolhouse was on School Street. Its unpainted clapboard walls had weathered to every shade of brown. Charlotte had seen the schoolhouse many times but had never been inside. She noticed an entryway with pegs for coats in winter and a shelf where Tom stowed the dinner basket next to lots of other baskets.

An open doorway led to the large schoolroom. In the front of the room was a raised platform, upon which sat Miss Heath's desk. There was a fireplace on one wall, clean and empty now for summer. The other three walls were lined with rough wooden desks, bearing scars and ink stains from the pupils of years past. The high benches that went with the desks had no backs, so that the students could sit facing either way—toward the desks and walls or into the center of the room. The desks were for the older students, Tom told her, taking a seat at one of them next to some other boys his age.

Charlotte wasn't sure where she belonged. She was grateful when Miss Heath told her to sit in an outside row, with the primer class. There were two other children in that class: a thin, shaggy-haired boy who shared a bench with his older brother, and a girl Charlotte's age sitting all by herself.

"Sit there beside Susan, Charlotte," Miss Heath said, pointing to the empty spot beside the girl. Charlotte sat with the desk behind her, facing into the center of the room, like the rest of the older children.

Charlotte saw a great many children whom she knew from church, or from calling on neighbors with Mama. But she had never before seen the girl beside her. While Miss Heath made a short welcoming speech, Charlotte tried to steal a look at her seatmate without letting on that she was doing so. All she got was a glimpse of very clean apron over faded pink calico, and the sudden impression that the girl was openly studying her. Quickly Charlotte looked away and pretended to be listening to Miss Heath with all her might.

But after Miss Heath had said the morning prayer, the girl whispered to Charlotte, "I have a plum tart in my dinner basket. You can have some if you like."

"Oh!" said Charlotte, surprised. "You can have some of my cookies," she added hastily so the girl wouldn't think she was greedy. "Only I think my brother broke them up."

"That's all right," Susan whispered. "They taste *almost* as good that way."

"Yes, *almost*," Charlotte said, and she smiled. She knew all at once that they were going to be friends.

At dinnertime, they found a spot together on the grassy slope beside the schoolhouse, beneath a stand of silvery birches. Tom came running up and made impatient noises while Charlotte unfolded the red-and-white napkin.

"Hurry up," he said crossly. "The other fellows will be done eating by the time I get there."

He snatched up his share of the bread and cheese. Beneath them was a jumble of broken cookies.

Charlotte glared at Tom reproachfully. He shrugged as if to say it didn't matter, but his eyes looked sorry.

"Here," he said carelessly, "this one is almost whole. You can have it."

He picked out his share of cookie pieces and ran off to join the other boys his age, calling back over his shoulder, "Don't throw out the crumbs—I'll eat 'em later!"

Charlotte rolled her eyes. But Susan laughed and said, "You're awfully lucky to have a brother."

"Don't you?" Charlotte asked.

"No, nor any sisters, either," the girl said. Charlotte couldn't think of anyone else she knew who was the only child in the family.

Who did Susan play with? Charlotte felt suddenly very glad to have so many brothers and sisters—even a brother like Tom, who would as soon eat a pile of crumbs off a napkin as a nice, whole, round cookie.

"I'd give anything for a sister," Susan said. "If I had one, her name would be Emmeline."

"Oh, how lovely!" said Charlotte.

Susan had brown eyes and silky brown hair, straight as a pin, that she wore tucked behind her ears. When she laughed, which was often, her hair slipped out and fell into her eyes.

Her father was a merchant who owned three ships. He used to bring home peppermints and other candies all the time. But now, Susan told Charlotte importantly, times were hard because of the war.

"It's the blockade," she explained. Charlotte nodded solemnly. Susan told her that his ships had been docked for months, because the British navy would not let them out of Boston Harbor. Until last week, Susan had lived in Boston, but now her family had come to stay with her uncle on Centre Street. He was a tinsmith, and Susan's father had come to work in his shop.

Miss Heath came out then and rang the bell. Reluctantly Susan and Charlotte stood and folded up their napkins. It was so pleasant sitting out in the speckled shade of the birches, amid the soft grass and the yellow dandelions bright as suns.

C Is for Coach

When lessons began, Susan did not have a primer to study from, so Charlotte shared hers. She held it half on her lap and half on Susan's so they could both see.

Miss Heath told them to study the first two pages. There was a verse at the top, and below it were the ABCs, each letter in a little box with a picture and a word that went with it. Miss Heath read them the verse and said they must learn it by heart before the end of the week.

It went:

He that ne'er learns his A, B, C,
For ever will a Blockhead be;
But he that learns these Letters fair
Shall have a Coach to take the Air.

They repeated it two or three times after Miss Heath, until they began to know it by heart. Then she left them and said she must give Freddy Tanner his lesson. He was the shaggy-haired boy in the primer class with them, but he studied from a different book.

While Miss Heath was with Freddy, Charlotte and Susan had to sit still and be quiet. They stared at the pictures below their verse. Charlotte knew the names of some of the letters, and she thought she could see how they went with the words and pictures: *A for Apple, B for Bull, C for Cat.*

Then Miss Heath went over to the other side of the room to give an arithmetic lesson to Tom's class. Charlotte and Susan stared at the primer as if they were studying, and whispered to each other.

Long before the week was out, both girls knew the verse by heart. Miss Heath called them to the front of the room and made them recite it to the class. They both got through it perfectly.

During the next week, there was far less whispering on Charlotte and Susan's bench than there might otherwise have been. Miss Heath had said they must learn the whole alphabet. When they knew all the letters and the words that went with them, they would stand up and recite those.

The girls bent over the primer, their two heads close enough to touch, staring hard at the letters and the helpful pictures that went with each one. *D for Dog, E for Egg,* Charlotte mouthed silently, and Susan's lips moved noiselessly behind the curtain of her hair.

At last came the day when Miss Heath called them up to recite. Charlotte and Susan squeezed each other's hands. They went to stand beside the teacher's desk.

"Charlotte, you first," said Miss Heath.

Charlotte took a deep breath. Her stomach felt fluttery. She hated to stand up here with everyone staring at her.

"A for Apple," she began. She made it all the way to "J for Judge" without any difficulty, but then she caught a glimpse of Abner Dickinson in the back of the room. He was gaping at her with his eyes crossed and his mouth twisted into a hideous grimace. It was such an ugly face that Charlotte's mind went blank for a moment. She knew what letter came next—she *did* know it—but that face!

Then Tom saw what Abner was doing and socked him on the shoulder. Tom might make all the faces he liked at his own sister, but no one else had better try it.

Charlotte smiled at him gratefully. "K for King," she said, because of course she had known it all along.

"L for Lion, M for Mouse, N for Nag." She did not falter again until "Y," which always stumped her because the picture in the book did not, in her opinion, make any sense.

She closed her eyes hard and saw the picture

in her mind. It was a lamb, but she must not say "Y for Lamb." That was not it. . . .

"Y for Young Lamb!" she cried triumphantly. That was it. As if there was any such thing as an *old* lamb!

"And Z for Zany," she finished. The picture for that one was a court jester, with bells on his hat. Charlotte could see it clearly in her mind's eye, and she felt as if the bells were ringing for her, for she had made it all the way through!

She turned her attention to Susan, who was just about to begin. She started out strong, just as Charlotte had, but then, there was one terrifying moment when she came to a dead stop and her eyes looked wild. Charlotte had to bite her lip to stop herself from calling out what came next. But at last, Susan gulped and gave a little jump, and the words burst out of her.

"X for Xerxes!" That was the one Susan always had the most trouble with; she had often complained to Charlotte that the crowned man in the drawing could be any old king, and that his name might just as easily have been George or John as Xerxes. But she had remembered at last, and her voice soared as she finished. "Y for Young Lamb—Z FOR ZANY!"

"Goodness," Miss Heath said, blinking. "Very good, Susan, but you must remember that a young lady never shouts."

"Yes, ma'am!" Susan said in a voice that stopped just short of being a shout itself. Charlotte grinned at her; she was so glad that both of them had made it through.

Charlotte had a very grownup feeling when she and Susan walked home together after school. Their shadows stretched ahead of them on the road.

"Look," Charlotte said suddenly. "Our shadows. They're like grown-up ladies."

"Oh!" Susan cried. "They are! Only the skirts are too short. Grown-up ladies would wear longer skirts."

"And bonnets," Charlotte admitted. But it was still fun to watch the shadows and pretend they were themselves, all grown up.

"When I'm grown up," Charlotte declared, "I'm going to have lots of bonnets and a coach all my own. You and I can drive around all day."

"Will your husband let you do that?" Susan asked.

"He'll have to," said Charlotte. "Or I won't let *him* ride in it."

"Oh, Charlotte, that's a lovely plan," said Susan admiringly. She smiled at Charlotte and locked arms with her. On the road their shadows locked arms, too, tall and slender and graceful as ladies. It was hard for Charlotte to believe that there had ever been a time when she hadn't wanted to go to school.

Emmeline

One July day a mysterious thing happened: Susan suddenly cried out in surprise during lessons. Everyone turned to look at her; Miss Heath's eyebrows made questioning points on her brow.

"What is it, Susan?"

"I—I beg your pardon," Susan stammered. "It's just that I saw my cousin Frank coming—and here he is."

And indeed, a young man had just entered the room, ducking his head apologetically. He glanced at Susan and then hurried to speak to

Miss Heath. Miss Heath's puzzled expression changed to one of concern.

"Yes, indeed, I'll see to it," she told the young man. He thanked her and strode back toward the door, giving Susan a little wave as he went.

Susan's eyes were wide and bewildered. She waited for Miss Heath to explain. Charlotte felt her own heart beating with worry—suppose something had happened? Things did happen sometimes. Mothers took sick; fathers fell off ladders. Perhaps something had happened to one of Susan's father's ships, up at the harbor in Boston. . . .

But all Miss Heath said was "Susan, your cousin says you're to go home with Charlotte for the night."

Susan and Charlotte looked at each other in disbelief. This was certainly nothing Charlotte would have guessed. How lovely to think of having Susan spend the night in her house! But it was odd, too, and she could see that Susan was worried.

"Please, ma'am," Susan asked, "is anything wrong?"

Miss Heath paused a moment, then shook her head. She would not say anything more about it, except to tell Susan not to worry and that her father would explain everything tomorrow.

After that it seemed as if a week had passed before Miss Heath stood and said, "School is dismissed." Charlotte and Susan hurried out the door and down the road. They went so fast that Tom did not catch up to them until they reached the mill.

"Do you think your mother will know what's happened?" Susan asked Charlotte.

Tom shrugged. "It's likely. She knows most everything that's going on. Maybe your house burned down," he added helpfully.

Susan gasped, and her eyes looked frantic. "Tom!" cried Charlotte angrily. She grabbed Susan's hand, and together they sprinted past the smithy and across Tide Mill Lane to the house. Mama and Lydia were out beside the garden wall, folding up linen sheets that had been spread out to bleach in the sun all day. Mary stood holding on to the wall nearby, her long white frock trailing in the dirt.

Charlotte and Susan ran to Mama and pulled at her dress, speaking both at once. Mama laughed and told them to calm down. Then she put a hand on Susan's head and said, "Dinna work yourself into a lather, lass. Your papa was here not an hour gone, and he said to tell you your mother's just a mite under the weather. We shall have us a grand time tonight, and in the mornin', he'll come for you."

Her smile was so warm that Charlotte did not feel worried anymore.

"Will my mother be all right?" Susan asked, twisting her apron between her hands.

"You must do as your papa says, child, and not worry yourself," Mama said gently. Then she told them to run and play until tea.

Charlotte and Susan took Mary by the hands and, holding her gown out of the way, led her to a flat stretch of ground beyond the garden. Mary went on wobbly, stumbling legs, for she had only just begun to walk. Charlotte gave her the clothespin doll to play with.

Suddenly Susan cried, "Mary, no!" and

lunged toward the baby. Mary had the doll's head in her mouth and was sucking happily. Charlotte ran to rescue her poor doll from the sticky mouth, causing Mary to wail in outrage.

"Mary, how could you!" she yelled. "If her face is gone . . ."

But it was all right. The paint had not rubbed off; the red mouth still smiled, and the black eyes stared as cheerfully as ever. There were only two little dents on the back of the glossy head to show that Mary had gotten at it.

"She left *bite* marks," Charlotte fumed.

"You can hardly see them," Susan said kindly. "It's lucky her hair is dark."

Mary wouldn't stop crying, so they took her back to Mama and Lydia. Mama lifted the baby to her hip and said, "There, there, my little one. You'll get on better in life if you learn not to eat other mothers' children."

That made everyone giggle. Charlotte kissed her doll and stroked her poor dented head.

"Aren't you *ever* going to name her?" Lydia asked.

"Of course I am!" Charlotte was indignant.

"I just haven't found the perfect name yet."

Susan climbed on top of the garden wall and tried to walk around it. After a few steps, she wobbled and fell off. It was all right, for the wall was low. Charlotte had fallen off it lots of times, but she almost never fell now, for she had had a lot of practice. She showed Susan how to stretch out her arms to keep her balance. The sun-warmed pudding stone felt hot on their bare feet.

"Why is it called pudding stone, Mama?" Charlotte asked.

"Whisht! Have I never told you that story?" Mama cried. "I canna believe it." She sat right down on the warm stone wall, with Mary in her lap.

"A long, long time ago, there was a giant livin' here wi' his family. He was so big that the whole of Roxbury Common could fit in his front parlor.

"This giant, he had him a wife and three children: a girl in the middle and a boy at each end. You never saw such a spoiled lot in all your life.

"Now one day the wife, she thought she'd

· 89 ·

give the children a treat for dinner. She mixed up a pudding. She brought it to the table and dished up a helping for each of her children.

"The oldest child looked in the youngest child's bowl, and he cried out, ''Tisn't fair—you've given him more!' So the giant's wife put a little more pudding in the oldest child's dish.

"Then the middle child cried out, ''Tisn't fair—you've given him more!' So the wife put a little more pudding in her dish.

"Then the youngest cried out, ''Tisn't fair—you've given her more!' And at that, the wife gave up tryin' and plopped the pudding pan on the table.

"'You may serve yourselves,' she said, and she left the room.

"The three of them yanked and they tugged and they pulled that bowl back and forth between them. They pulled so hard that the bowl went flyin' out of all their hands and sailed right through the open window.

"Now remember, this was a giant's bowl, and sure it was a giant's pudding. There was enough of it there to feed an army of folks like us. Pudding went this way and pudding went that way. You canna imagine the mess. From here to Dorchester, the land was covered with lumps o' pudding. The bowl landed upside down right over yon, where Great Hill is, wi' a big mess o' pudding still clingin' to its sides.

"Well, when the giant's wife saw the mess, she said she'd have no part in clearin' it away. The children had made it, and the children must clean it up. But those naughty children, they never did wipe up their mess, and so those lumps of pudding stayed where they were.

"When night came, the lumps cooled off, and by morning they were hard as stone. And there they stayed, year after year—and there they are today.

"Whenever someone like your Papa wants to build a wall," Mama finished, "all he has to do is find himself a good lump o' pudding."

"I know what Great Hill is!" Charlotte cried. "It's the upside-down bowl!"

"Aye," said Mama. "Away on the other side o' Great Hill there's a quarry, where folks have dug right through to the pudding inside. Roxbury pudding stone is known up and down New England, it is."

That night was like a holiday, with Susan tucked between Charlotte and Lydia in their bed, her hands covered up by the too-long sleeves of Lydia's last-year's nightgown. They whispered and giggled until Mama came in to say they were making so much noise, she had no doubt the cows were having trouble sleeping out in the barn.

"Shall I sing you to sleep?" she asked. When they eagerly said yes, she sat and sang a low, sweet song she had learned as a girl in Scotland.

> "Come all ye men and maidens and list unto
>   my rhyme,
>   'Twas all about a damsel who was scarcely
>   in her prime;
>   She beat the blushin' roses and admired by
>   all around
>   Was lovely young Caroline of Edinboro
>   Town."

The candle flickered, and Charlotte lay watching the shadows it made until her eyes closed. Mama's voice was soft as a kiss.

The next morning Susan was helping Charlotte wipe the breakfast dishes when Susan's father burst into the kitchen.

"I beg your pardon, Mrs. Tucker," Mr. Custer panted. "That is—good day. I—er—how do you do?"

He took off his hat and put it back on again, and then took it off and laid it absently on the table, in the middle of the floury spot where Mama had been rolling out a piecrust. He was a large, heavyset man who looked more like a farmer than a merchant, with his powerful arms and his shirtsleeves rolled up.

Mama smiled and greeted him warmly. She studied his face and said softly, "I trust all is well?"

Mr. Custer grinned broadly. "Indeed it is!" He went to Susan and caught her up in a bear hug. "And how's my little lady?" he asked. "Shall we go home and see who's come to visit your mama?"

"Who is it?" Susan asked, but Charlotte suddenly realized what he meant.

"A baby!" she cried. She remembered a distant time when Mrs. John Heath had come and taken Charlotte and Lydia and the boys to her big white house on the other side of the hill beyond the garden. Miss Heath—she had been Amelia then—had given Charlotte a doughnut to eat. Later Charlotte had been set atop a gray horse that stood quietly munching oats; and then Papa had come and told them all they had a new sister at home; and that was how Mary had come to live with them.

She dropped her dishcloth and squeezed Susan's hand. "You're a big sister!"

"Truly?" Susan stared at her father.

Beaming, he nodded. "She's hit the nail on the head, Charlotte has. Clever girl!"

"Oh, Papa!" cried Susan, clasping her hands. "What is her name to be? Oh, please, might we call her Emmeline?"

Mr. Custer threw back his head and laughed.

"We might, my dear—but I don't think *he* would thank you for it when he got older."

Susan froze. "He?" she asked.

"Why, yes, it's a fine hearty boy! We shall call him Robert, after my father."

Susan looked so surprised that everyone laughed.

"Don't worry," Charlotte told her. "Brothers are nice, too."

"I know." Susan sighed. "But I did want to have a sister so I could call her Emmeline."

Charlotte nodded sympathetically. Robert was a nice enough name, but it was nothing compared to Emmeline.

Then she jumped, and her hand went to her apron pocket. "Suppose—" she said, taking out the clothespin doll and cradling her tenderly, "suppose we call *her* Emmeline! But only if you want to," she added.

Susan smiled. "It's perfect," she said.

POUNDED CHEESE

September came, and Charlotte's very first school term was over. One afternoon, she went into the kitchen and found Mama furiously pounding a cheese with a mortar and pestle. With each stroke, she thumped the pestle against the mortar so hard, the table shook beneath it. Mama's eyes snapped with anger, and there were bright red spots on her cheeks.

Charlotte could see that she was angry about something Lydia was reading from a newspaper.

Lydia's voice was impatient and bored. She

did not like reading aloud. She looked up eagerly when Mama threw down her pestle and said, "I've heard enough, Lydia. Your father will be wantin' to hear this when he comes in, and I dinna think I can stomach it twice."

Lydia sighed with relief. Charlotte came to stand at the edge of the table. Mama scraped the creamy softened cheese out of the mortar into a mixing bowl. Her spoon made a clattering sound against the mortar, which was like a shallow stone bowl. Mama took another chunk of cheese that had been cut from one of the big round cheeses in the cellar and put it into the mortar.

"Charlotte, fetch a cloth to cover that bowl. The flies will be all over it," Mama said. Her voice was still sharp and angry. "Settin' fire to our own capital city! 'Tis barbaric!" Mama pounded the cheese so hard, Charlotte thought the mortar would crack in two. Lydia, catching Charlotte's eye, made a little worried grimace.

"Boston's on fire?" Charlotte asked, horrified. All those houses she had seen from the Neck—and the copper dome of the State

House gleaming in the sunlight—suppose they had burned down!

But Mama looked up from her pounding, and her angry gaze softened. "Och, nay, darlin', not Boston. 'Tis Washington City they've burned, those scoundrels. The capital of the United States! Their navy sailed right up the Potomac and landed an army. Set fire to the President's house, they did!" She was still angry, but it was a kind of bold, defiant anger that made Charlotte feel somehow safe. Nothing bad could happen in Roxbury as long as Mama and Papa were here.

"Mama!" Lewis came running into the kitchen, his hair sticking up wildly on his head. "Have you heard? The British—"

Mama cut him off, nodding grimly. "Aye. I went to Bacon's for coffee—not that there was anything decent, thanks to that cursed blockade—such low-quality stuff I've never seen in all me life." *Thump, thump* went the pestle in the mortar. "But the place was packed to the gills with folks talkin' about the attack." As she spoke, she scraped the rest of the pounded cheese into the redware bowl.

Lewis's eyes shone with excitement. "I wish I'd been there—I'd have given them what for!"

"Lewis Tucker!" Mama cried. "Bite your tongue, lad! I thank heaven you're too young for any militia to take you."

Lewis, avoiding her eye, gave a heavy sigh. Mama turned toward the mantel shelf to take down the spices for the cheese, and Lewis took the opportunity to relieve his feelings by making a face at Lydia behind Mama's back. Lydia opened her mouth to tattle, then thought better of it and snapped her mouth shut.

Mama brought jars of pepper and curry to the table. Charlotte watched as she sprinkled the spices generously into the creamy cheese. The smell of the curry powder made Charlotte's mouth water. Pounded cheese was one of her favorite dishes. Mama had learned the recipe from a neighbor lady last year; it was exotic and rich, and since spices were so expensive because of the war, it was not a dish Mama made very often.

"Papa sent me over to tell you he and Will

won' be home until late tonight," Lewis said. "He says you aren't to hold tea for him. Half the neighborhood has come in wanting some ironwork done today."

Mama snorted. "Ironwork, my eye. What they want is a place to stand around jawin' about the attack, that's what." She shook black pepper into the bowl, and the cayenne that was red as her own hair. It made a dust cloud above the mixing bowl. "They'll be there past dark, drainin' our cider barrels and shoutin' about how if only *they'd* been in Washington City last week, Mrs. Madison wouldna have had to watch her house burn down."

She fixed Lewis with a fierce glare, for he had all but said the same thing. He ducked his head and nodded sheepishly. But then his face grew sober and he said, "I don't care if I *am* too young to join the militia, Mama. If the British come here, I'll fight them anyway, before I'll let them set fire to our house."

Mama's eyes grew gentle. "Aye, lad, I know you would. But it'll not come to that. There's no reason in the world for the British to attack

Boston—not with half our merchants doin' trade wi' them on the sly, the rogues." The fierce note had come back into her voice. "I'm no supporter of this war, either, but I'd never go behind me own country's back to sell to the enemy."

Lewis nodded. He seemed to Charlotte to have grown suddenly very much older. He stood nearly as tall as Mama. Charlotte felt a little awed by him. He knew as much about the war as a grown-up.

Lewis must have felt her staring at him, for he looked her way. He winked at her and said he must get back to the shop.

"Tell your father I'll send their suppers out to the smithy," Mama said. "I'll not have anyone starvin' to death just because the British have no decency."

When it was time to wash hands and faces and set the table, Mama asked Lewis to say grace, since Papa wasn't there. Then she passed around the platter of slices of bread spread thickly with the creamy, spicy pounded cheese.

Charlotte took a big bite. She had chewed

and swallowed it before the burning began—
a spicy fire that made her gasp and brought
tears to her eyes. It didn't taste like any pounded
cheese she'd had before. Lydia clapped a hand
to her mouth, and Lewis let out a muffled shout.
He grabbed his mug of cider and gulped
it down. Tom was chewing slowly, a funny,
strained look on his face.

Mama had been spooning cold porridge
into Mary's mouth, but now she stopped and
looked around the table in surprise.

"What in heaven?" she said, staring per-
plexed at Tom's watering eyes and at Lewis fan-
ning his mouth with his hand.

"Whatever is the matter wi' you children?"
Mama asked.

"The cheese, Mama," Lewis muttered. "It's
a little . . ." He trailed off.

"What about it?" Mama asked, but Lewis
only shrugged apologetically.

"I think . . . I think there's too much
cayenne, Mama," said Lydia.

"What? Nonsense."

Charlotte remembered how the red powder

had made a dust cloud over the bowl. Lydia was right. But Charlotte was not going to be the one to tell Mama that.

"It's not so bad, Mama," said Lewis. "Just caught me by surprise, that's all."

"That's right, Mama," said Tom, and he bravely took another big bite. But it made him cough and gasp until Mama had to pour him another mugful of cider.

"Good Lord, how bad can it be?" said Mama, and she tasted a little of the cheese. Her face turned red.

"Great lairds of thunder!" she cried. "We canna eat this! It wouldna be fit for a pig, if we had one!"

She stood abruptly, her chair scraping against the floor behind her. "Pass me your plates, everyone. It's those blast—those confounded British. I was that distracted about the attack, I didna know whether I was comin' or goin', making supper."

Quickly around the table she went, scraping the bread and cheese onto a plate. "It's bread and butter for us tonight, my dears. But first—" She looked around the table with a gleam in her eye. "Follow me."

Mama led them all out to the garden, back to a far corner where mint had escaped its tidy patch, spreading in a fragrant tangle along the stone wall. Night was falling; orange beams slanted toward the earth beneath gray billows of cloud.

"Fetch a spade, Lewis," Mama said, and Lewis ran to the lean-to while Mama cleared a space on the ground by pulling up the mint in great handfuls. The air was drowned in the smell of mint.

Charlotte and Lydia and Tom stood in a half ring around Mama, Mary wriggling on Lydia's hip. A light wind laughed in the tops of the maple trees, then raced off to wrap itself in the smoke of a hearth fire. An owl screeched somewhere over the sheep pasture. Charlotte knew from the sound that it was the barn owl that lived above the haymow.

The rattling leaves and the cool, sharp air whispered of autumn, and Charlotte realized suddenly that she was cold in her thin summer dress. But nothing in the world could have made her go inside just then.

Lewis came back with the spade. Mama took it and, kneeling, dug a hole in the earth. The good musty smell of soil mingled with the mint and the wood smoke.

"What are you going to do, Mama?" Tom asked. Laughing, Mama murmured, "From dust ye come and to dust ye shall return." She scraped the pounded cheese into the hole. Charlotte gasped, for though she had guessed what Mama meant to do, it still surprised her. Food must never be wasted, *never*. The cheese had been ruined past eating, but Charlotte knew that some mothers would have made their children force it down, just to keep it from going to waste.

Mama heaped dirt over the pale mess in the hole, and then she said, "Pack it well in. I'll not have cheese sourin' in my garden after the next rain."

For a moment none of them moved.

Charlotte looked at Lydia, and Lydia looked at Charlotte. Tom stared wide-eyed at Mama, and it was Lewis who finally stepped onto the mound of soil and began to stomp his legs up and down.

"Is that the best you can do?" teased Mama, and she stepped forward and began to dance a little jig on top of the buried cheese.

"Give us a tune, Lydia," she said.

So Lydia sang her favorite song, about a farmer and his dog.

> *"A farmer he had a pretty little dog,*
> *Called his name 'Old Bingo,'*
> *B-I-N-G-O,*
> *Called his name 'Old Bingo'!"*

Lewis held out his hands to Charlotte. She grabbed them, and he danced her round and round, singing along with Lydia in his loud, exuberant voice. Tom took Mama's hands, and Lydia whirled in circles with Mary in her arms.

"B with an I, I with an N, N with a G,
G with an O,
B-I-N-G-O,
Called his name 'Old Bingo'!"

The scent of crushed mint was thick as a cloak. Their voices rang out in the quiet air; it was as if even the birds had hushed to listen to them. Charlotte wondered if Papa could hear them down in the smithy. Perhaps if they sang louder, even the British would hear them in far-off Washington City and would know not to come near, not to so much as set a foot in the direction of Roxbury.

The sun slipped below the feathery line of the trees beyond Mr. Heath's back pasture. Night had fallen, but Mama went on dancing, so the rest of them did, too.

IN THE SMITHY

Sometimes, during the bright cold after-noons of fall, Charlotte ran across the road to the smithy, to watch Papa and Will at work. Its whitewashed walls gleamed like snow against the scarlet and golden leaves of the trees that bordered Mr. Heath's back pasture. Gray smoke swirled up from the chimney, and the roar of the forge was louder than the wind.

When she crept into the shop, Charlotte felt shy, for there were always so many people inside. Papa's customers liked to stay and talk, trading stories and news.

Often there were three or four of Tom's friends as well, playing in the open doorway and pretending to be blacksmiths themselves. They envied Tom, for he had chores to do inside the shop. Tom pushed his broom around importantly and made a show of straightening the tools upon the shelf.

Charlotte didn't see what was so impressive about sweeping and tidying up. She did it at home every day of the year, and no one ever came to watch *her* at work.

But she understood why the boys liked to watch Papa and Will. It was exciting to see them use their hammers and pincers to twist and shape the hot iron as if it were taffy. The muscles stood out on Papa's arms, and drops of sweat ran down his face. When he wiped his forehead with the back of an arm, he left black streaks above his eyebrows.

What Charlotte liked best of all was watching Papa put on a set of horseshoes. The horses were like people, every one different; but Papa knew them all. He spoke to them in Gaelic, the language he had grown up with in Scotland,

and it was as if it were a secret language known only by Papa and horses. Their ears pricked up and followed Papa as he went from leg to leg, lifting each one gently while he looked for cracks in the hooves.

When Papa made new horseshoes, he started with a long, thin bar of pig iron and heated it on the hot coals. When the black iron turned red, it was melted enough to be cut. With his great pincers, Papa snipped off a piece just the right size for a shoe. He made it look as easy as cutting butter with a knife.

He began to shape the short piece into a shoe. Again he laid it on the coals, and when it glowed red, he used his long-handled tongs to remove it. He struck the iron with a hammer, slowly bending it to the right shape. Every time the hammer crashed down, sparks flew off the iron, shining in the air like lightning bugs.

In and out of the coals the iron went, until at last it looked like a proper horseshoe. He made all four shoes, one after another.

While Papa worked, Will would attend to the customers who streamed in and out of the smithy, bringing in tools to be repaired, or asking for a new set of andirons for the fireplace, or a spider-legged pot to set over the coals of a kitchen hearth.

Will liked to talk as he worked, and his strong voice carried over the roar of the fire and the clang of his hammer on the hot iron. He kept up a running conversation with the men who leaned against the walls discussing the war, or the price of sugar, or Chester Hutchinson's three-legged pig.

While they talked, Lewis hurried about, keeping the water barrel full, putting more coal on the fire, and fetching tools for Papa and Will. And all the time, he was hanging on every word the men said.

One day Mr. Davis, who Charlotte knew from church, came in waving a newspaper.

"The British attacked Baltimore!" he shouted.

Lewis stood frozen with his broom in his hand.

"Baltimore!" he cried.

Charlotte wasn't sure where Baltimore was, but it seemed to be near Washington City, which

Charlotte knew wasn't too close. She must not be frightened.

"Yes, but we held them off. A man named Mr. Key wrote a fine account of the battle in the paper," Mr. Davis said. "He was there all night, watching the British blast Fort McHenry. For all he could tell, it was a pile of rubble."

"Heaven to Pete," murmured Will.

"You said it," agreed Mr. Davis. "Key said he like to cried the next morning. But when the sun came up, he saw our flag still flying over the fort. Then he knew we'd won the battle and everything would be all right."

"I wish I'd been there!" Lewis said longingly.

"Well, young man, this Mr. Key—seems he's something of a poet, too. He went home and wrote some verses about what happened. You hear them, feels like you *are* there, standing right beside him on the deck of that ship." He held up the newspaper again. "Every paper in the country is printing it this week. It's called 'Defense of Fort McHenry.'"

"Let's hear it, Davis," said one of the other men.

Mr. Davis nodded, and he unfolded the news sheet and read:

"Oh! say, can you see, by the dawn's
early light,
What so proudly we hailed at the twilight's
last gleaming?
Whose broad stripes and bright stars,
through the perilous fight,
O'er the ramparts we watched were so
gallantly streaming?
And the rockets' red glare, the bombs
bursting in air,
Gave proof through the night that our flag
was still there.
Oh! say, does that star-spangled banner
yet wave
O'er the land of the free and the home of
the brave?"

Mr. Davis was right. Though Charlotte did not understand all of it, the rockets, the bombs—she could see them flashing in the sky like the fireworks on Independence Day. And she saw the flag with its fifteen white stars glowing over Fort McHenry. Papa wiped his eyes.

"Ah, that's grand," he said.

"Yes, it is," said Mr. Davis. "This Francis Key is a fine poet. My hired man says folks have set it to music already—you know that old air 'To Anacreon in Heaven'? That's the tune. Fits these verses like it was made for them."

Papa nodded. He knew the song. That evening he brought home a copy of the newspaper and asked Mama to sing the verses.

The parlor fire crackled and the wind beat on the windowpanes. Charlotte and Lydia sat with clasped hands, and the boys stopped in the middle of their game of jackstraws to listen. Mary was asleep in Papa's lap, her little mouth pushed into an O against his shoulder.

Will sat near the fire with his chair tipped back, staring at the flames, his brown eyes serious and shadowed.

The candle burning on the table beside Mama's chair cast a yellow glow across her and made her red hair glow like fire. Her voice rang out like a bell.

"Oh! thus be it ever when freemen
    shall stand
Between their loved home
    and the war's desolation,
Blest with vict'ry and peace,
    may the Heav'n-rescued land
Praise the Pow'r that hath made
    and preserved us a nation.
Then conquer we must,
    when our cause it is just,
And this be our motto,
    'In God is our trust.'
And the star-spangled banner in triumph
    shall wave
O'er the land of the free and the home
    of the brave."

Apple Time

In October, four of Papa's customers paid him in apples. Mama sent a great many of them to Mr. Heath, to be made into cider in his cider press; she kept a basket of russets in the kitchen for the children to eat.

Charlotte ran outdoors in the crisp autumn air with apples and Emmeline bouncing in her apron pockets.

Tom ate a dozen green apples on a dare and got so sick he spent three days in bed. After that, he wouldn't eat apples for a month, not even when Mama served apple pie with dinner.

Mama shrugged and said that left more pie for the rest of them.

Even after apple pie and cider and all the apples eaten out in the yard or munched at night before the fire, there were bushels of apples left. These must be peeled and cored and sliced, and hung to dry. Charlotte thought that was the very best thing about apples, for it meant apple-paring parties.

So Mama sent word to the ladies of the neighborhood that she was having a paring the next evening after tea. Will had an errand on Centre Street, and Mama asked him to stop at the tin shop and leave word for Susan's mother. Charlotte could hardly sleep that night, wondering if Susan would come. She had barely seen her since school had ended, except for a few minutes before and after church.

Susan did come. Her mother brought the baby, too, well wrapped in bunting.

"Goodness, such a little dear!" Mama said, kissing his cheeks.

Susan rolled her eyes at Charlotte. "I don't see why everyone makes such a fuss," she whispered. "He doesn't *do* anything, except sleep and eat and cry."

"At least he doesn't try to eat your doll," Charlotte said. But they only pretended not to like their babies. Really they liked them very much.

The parlor was so full of people—and apples—there was hardly room to move. But quickly all the ladies settled into chairs and took up the knives they'd brought from home. The confusion of noise subsided to a loud, laughing murmur of gossip and news.

Charlotte and Susan sat squeezed together on a little bench. They talked and talked, and watched the ladies move quickly through the baskets of apples, peeling and coring and slicing them.

Lydia and some other big girls had been given needles and string, and they strung the apple slices on long strands that Papa and Will hung from the rafters. The apples would hang there in merry festoons until they were well dried out. This was how Mama made the apples last through the year, for dried apples kept far longer than fresh ones.

Miss Heath and some of the other young ladies played a game with their apple peels. They cut the peel off in one long, spiraling piece, and when they were done, they closed their eyes and threw the peels over their shoulders. Then they looked to see if the peels had fallen to the floor in the shape of a letter. Miss Heath's peel looked like an *S*, and that meant she would marry a man whose first name started with *S*. Miss Heath blushed when she saw it, and made a face that was meant to look angry but wasn't really.

Miss Hannah Stowe, the cooper's oldest daughter, said teasingly, "Oh, what a pity Sam Dudley isn't here; I hear tell he threw an apple peel and it spelled 'A'!" Then Miss Heath blushed all the more.

Charlotte thought it was a very silly game. Apple snap was much more fun. Will tied a whole apple to a string and hung it from the ceiling. Each child had a turn at trying to take a bite out of the apple without using hands.

Tom was the best at getting bites. He got the

most bites, but Lydia got the biggest. Mary stood beneath the apple with her arms outstretched, crying, "Me, me, me!" until Lewis picked her up for a try. She was too little to understand the game; she grabbed at the apple with her chubby hands and pulled it right off the string. She looked so pleased with herself that no one could be angry with her, and Mama said it went to show that sometimes the smallest could be mightiest.

It was a lovely, laughing evening, and when it was over, Charlotte thought nothing could be half as much fun, ever again. But then, the following Saturday night, the molasses father came back to the table. For two whole days, Mama had boiled cider in the big iron kettle until it became thick and syrupy, and she said it was cider molasses. Charlotte was so glad to see the jolly father jug back in his place on the table. This was the Saturday family's last chance to be all together again for a long time, for the cows had stopped giving milk and there would be no more butter for the butter baby until spring.

With the molasses jug back where it belonged, Charlotte could almost forget there was a war going on at all. But that night, after supper, Papa said something to Mama that brought the war rushing back into the house like a gust of cold wind.

He came into the kitchen and pulled a chair up to the fire while Mama washed the dishes. Charlotte and Lydia hurried back and forth from the parlor, clearing the table.

Papa said, "The vote passed. Roxbury's militia is sending a unit up north to fight the British near Canada. Will's going with them on Monday noon."

Charlotte stood frozen before the kitchen cupboard with the molasses father in one hand and the vinegar mother in the other.

"Suppose we pack a picnic lunch and go to see him off?" Papa continued.

"Aye," Mama said, sliding a plate into the tin washpan. "Has a long march ahead of him, he does."

She gave a little sigh, and Papa nodded.

Lydia came in from the parlor with her

hands full of dishes. "What are you doing?" she asked Charlotte. "A snail would move faster."

"Will's leaving," Charlotte whispered.

Without even realizing it, Charlotte dropped the Saturday father. The little redware jug had slipped from her hand and crashed to the floor. It lay in pieces, and the molasses made a sticky pool on the sand.

Charlotte stared at it, horror-struck. Tears sprang to her eyes.

"What on earth?" Mama said, turning toward the cupboard with her dishcloth in hand. Papa half stood up from his chair.

Charlotte could not move. Lydia took the vinegar cruet from her hand, saying, "Here, you don't want to drop that, too," and all at once, Charlotte was sobbing and running.

She ran through the lean-to and out to the barn. Patience and Mollie looked up from their stalls with their mouths full of hay.

Charlotte climbed the ladder into the hay-mow, and threw herself down on the blanket of hay.

She heard steps upon the barn floor, and

then upon the rungs of the ladder, and she knew it was probably Lewis, sent to find her. Well, he could just go back inside. But a hand touched her hair, and it was not Lewis's hand. Charlotte raised her head to look. It was Mama, kneeling beside her in the hay with her skirts tucked up like a little girl. She didn't say a word, just sat Charlotte up and held her close as she smoothed the damp curls off her face.

For a long time, there was just the low grunting sound of the cows chewing their bites of hay. Then Mama said, "Would you believe I've never once been up here in all the years we've lived here?"

"Truly?" Charlotte said, in spite of herself. It was surprising to think that here was a place Charlotte came to before Mama did.

"Truly. 'Tis rather nice, is it not?"

Charlotte gave the tiniest, tiniest nod. She did not feel like agreeing that anything was nice, just now.

"Mama," she said, "is Will really going away?"

"Aye, that he is. I'm that proud of him, too. 'Tis a brave thing and a noble one, to fight for your country, Charlotte."

"But—" Charlotte groped for words, but all she could say was, "I don't want him to leave."

"Whisht, we mustn't think of ourselves just now, lass. I'll miss him, too, him wi' his rogue's smile and the manners of a king. And your papa will have a hard time findin' someone so clever and hardworkin' as Will to help him in the shop." Mama sighed. Her hands moved absently, picking bits of straw out of Charlotte's hair. "But Will feels he must go, and I must say I agree wi' him. I'd rather we'd stayed out of this war altogether, but we're in it now, and the army needs good brave lads like Will to kick those British soldiers back to England."

"Why are the British here, Mama? Why won't they leave us alone?"

"Well, as far as that goes," Mama said, "'tis America that declared war on England, not the other way round. Some people believe—President Madison is one of them—that America had no choice but to stand up to England and tell her she'd better think twice about tryin' to bully us—stealin' our sailors, sellin' guns to the Indians, and suchlike. We're a new country, you see, and we've got to show the world we're strong enough to look after ourselves. *That's* why we're at war, Charlotte. That's why Will is going to fight."

"Will he come back?" Charlotte asked. Her voice was very small.

Mama sighed again. "We must pray that he will, Lottie, and leave the rest to God. That is all I can tell you."

Charlotte balled up her fists in the hay and cried, "I hate this war! I hate it!"

"Hush, now," Mama said. "There's a great many folks feel that way, but you dinna hear them wailin' about it. Here you are in a fine snug house, safe and sound, wi' plenty o' food on the table. There's folks in Boston feelin' a much tighter pinch than we are, wi' their trade cut in half by the blockade. Not to mention all the poor souls down in Bladensburg, or up on the Niagara, who've had their homes burned out over their heads by British troops. We're that lucky, Charlotte Tucker, we ought to be on our knees every day thankin' God for what we've got."

But Charlotte did not feel the least bit thankful. She thought of the molasses, a dark pool spreading over the white sand on the floor.

"I broke the molasses jug," she said miserably.

"I know," Mama said. "We shall have to go to Bacon's and pick us out a new one."

"But it won't be the same!"

Mama shook her head gently. "Nay, lass, it willna be the same."

Will was going away. It didn't matter that the British would not come to Boston; Will was going to them. Nothing would be the same, not ever.

THE SEAGULL

On Monday morning, Will came home—only it was not his home, not anymore. He carried a lumpy burlap sack and an old musket that his father had used in the War for Independence many years ago.

There was no fire in the smithy's forge that day. It was a strange kind of morning that was not a workday and not a Sunday. Mama bustled about the kitchen packing a picnic lunch, and a separate bundle of food for Will in a checkered napkin. Will protested, saying his mother had already given him food enough for the whole army, but Mama ignored him, with a look in her eye that said wild horses couldn't stop her from sending Will off with some of her ginger cookies.

"Perhaps you should make me some pounded cheese, Mrs. Tucker," said Will, grinning wickedly. Of course he knew all about the cayenne disaster; Mama had told him and Papa herself. "If I could sneak it into the enemy's rations, they'd cry all the way back to England!"

"Whisht!" Mama said, tossing her head. "Give a lad a musket and he turns saucy on you!"

Charlotte did not see how anyone could make jokes today. She was not sure she wanted to go to the common to see Will off. But Mama said of course she must come; everyone must.

Lewis led the way past the smithy and the mill, toward the white spire of the meeting-house and the wide square of Roxbury Common. There was a great crowd there. Men in top hats stood importantly on the steps of the new town hall, looking out upon the soldiers in their untidy rows on the grass.

People milled in and out among the soldiers, saying good-bye. Mothers hugged lanky young men, who rolled their eyes with embarrassment but whose Adam's apples moved up and down in a swallowing, homesick kind of way. Fathers clapped their sons on the backs, and sweethearts held each other's hands.

Charlotte spotted Susan in the crowd. She waved, and Susan ran to join the Tuckers.

Will craned his neck around, searching for someone, and then his face lit up and he said, "Ah, there they are. Come, I want you all to meet my family."

He pushed through the crowd to a wagon standing on the roadside near the meetinghouse. A tall man with a wide-brimmed hat stood beside the horses; seated on the wagon box were two ladies in plain knitted shawls and straw bonnets. Will introduced them to Mama and Papa. The tall man was his father, and the older of the ladies was his mother. She had his same smiling eyes, and just now they gleamed with a proud light.

The younger lady was Will's Lucy. Charlotte

forgot that staring was impolite, and she stared so hard that Lydia had to nudge her before she remembered to curtsy. Then she blushed and curtsied hastily.

Lucy was not nearly as pretty as Miss Heath. She had a crooked mouth and a pale face that was marked with smallpox scars. But her smile was warm and lively, and her eyes were piercing blue. She leaned forward and gave Mama her hand.

"I'm so pleased to meet you, Mrs. Tucker," she said. "I've heard so much about all of you."

"And we of ye, as my mother's old cook used to say." Mama grinned. "I'm in the way of understandin' that we're to be neighbors when Will returns to us."

Lucy smiled again, this time at Will. "Yes, and I'm counting the days," she said frankly. Will smiled back.

Mama laughed and said, "I should think you would be!"

Lucy invited Charlotte and Susan to sit on the wagon seat with her for a spell. Papa lifted them up, and they looked out upon a sea of hats and bonnets. Charlotte had not known there were so many people in Roxbury.

"Look," called Lewis. "There's the captain. What's he shouting?"

"He's calling us to form ranks," Will said. Suddenly everyone was crowding around him to say good-bye. Charlotte hung back, but Will came to her and gave her shoulders a squeeze.

"I'll keep my eyes out for corbies when we march up north," he said. "You never know but one of them might take it into his head to have a look at the New World!"

Charlotte shook her head. "No, Will. You know they only live in Scotland."

"Ah, but the world is changing all the time, Charlotte," Will said, his voice gentle and low. "Just because something has always been one way, that doesn't mean it will go on being that way forever."

Charlotte knew he was talking about more than just corbies.

It was time for him to go. Taking up his

food bundles, he touched his hat and said, "Well, I'm off!" and strode away toward the lines of soldiers in the center of the common.

Mama wiped a tear from her eye, which surprised Charlotte. Mama never cried. The ache in Charlotte's throat was worse than crying. She looked for Will among the other soldiers but could not see him. The men looked all alike with their newly oiled muskets slung over their shoulders and their proud, determined faces staring straight ahead.

The captain, a stout man in a soldier's uniform, held up his sword. All the soldiers stood at attention in their rows.

Then the captain gave another signal, and the drummer began to play. Next to him, a soldier raised a fife to his lips. A shrill birdlike piping soared above the crowd. It was the tune of "Yankee Doodle," and its notes rang out clear and pure above the crowd. The soldiers began to march. They marched out of the grassy square and filed down Washington Street.

Past the town hall, past the grand houses

along the square, past Mr. Bacon's store they went, and the crowd of townspeople went behind them.

"Come, let's follow!" Susan cried, tugging Charlotte's hand. So they ran with the other children, following close behind the proudly marching soldiers.

When they reached the Neck, the crowd of children came to a stop. Charlotte stood on the side of the road, watching the soldiers march away toward Boston. The tide was in, making a bridge of the road. On both sides of the marching soldiers, the water stretched out broad and blue. Sunlight sparkled on the water and dazzled Charlotte's eyes. All around her the little waves glinted like the sun on the copper dome of the State House, across the bay at the edge of the sky.

All this time, Susan had been holding Emmeline. But now she slipped the doll back into Charlotte's hand. Charlotte squeezed Emmeline, hard. She didn't know how hard she was squeezing until Susan giggled and said,

"Lucky thing she's made from a clothespin and not a corn husk."

That made Charlotte laugh. She looked at Susan, and all at once she felt better. The war was taking Will away, and it had broken up the Saturday family. But if it hadn't been for the war, Susan would not have come to Roxbury. To think Charlotte might have sat alone on the bench all summer at school!

Charlotte could never choose between Will and Susan. She wouldn't want to. She began to see what Mama had meant about leaving things to God.

A seagull squawked from a fence post beside her. It might have been the same fence post and the same seagull Charlotte had seen before, the day she tried to walk to Scotland. The bird had a gray head and wings the color of old snow. It stared at Charlotte with a round, black eye. If Will were here, he could tell her what kind of seagull it was, and where it had started out, and where it was going. But the soldiers were halfway across the Neck now, growing smaller step by step.

The gull spread its pointed wings and soared into the air. Charlotte watched it sail high over the heads of the soldiers and out above the glittering water.

Keep your eye on Will, Charlotte told the bird. *And bring him back safe.* That made her think of the words of Mr. Key's song: "Oh! say, can you see . . . ?" Of course the gull could see, for it could fly so high that it was higher than Great Hill. It could watch over Will in the crowd of soldiers; it could see the whole of Boston. It could see the British frigates and sloops of war blocking the harbor, and Susan's father's ships waiting at the docks for the war to be won. It could go anywhere, see everything, and Charlotte wished with all her heart that she could go with it and see what *it* saw, out there in the wide world beyond Washington Street.

HISTORY: IN CHARLOTTE'S TIME

SONG: "BINGO"

GAME: APPLE SNAP

RECIPE: CORNMEAL PUDDING WITH MOLASSES

PREVIEW OF *ON TIDE MILL LANE*

IN CHARLOTTE'S TIME

Charlotte Tucker was born in 1809 in Roxbury, Massachusetts. What else was happening in America around that time?

1809 • James Madison inaugurated as fourth U.S. President

1810 • U.S. population 7.2 million

1812 • War of 1812 begins

1812 • The Brothers Grimm publish their Fairy Tales

1814 • British forces blockade Boston Harbor and burn Washington, D.C., and the White House

1814 • Francis Scott Key writes poem later set to music that becomes the U.S. National Anthem ("The Star-Spangled Banner")

1814 • Treaty of Ghent ends the War of 1812 on December 24

1817 • James Monroe inaugurated as fifth U.S. President

1820 • U.S. Population 9.6 million

1822 • Streets of Boston, MA, lit by gas light

1825 • John Quincy Adams inaugurated as sixth U.S. President

SONG

"BINGO"

Lewis held out his hands to Charlotte. She grabbed them, and he danced her round and round, singing with Lydia in his loud, exuberant voice.

"Bingo"

A farmer he had a pretty little dog,
Called his name 'Old Bingo,'
B-I-N-G-O,
Called his name 'Old Bingo'!
B with an I, I with an N, N with a G, G with an O,
B-I-N-G-O,
Called his name 'Old Bingo'!

That's the way Charlotte and Lewis sing the song, but you might know these lyrics instead.

"Bingo"

There was a farmer had a dog,
And Bingo was his name, oh!
B-I-N-G-O
B-I-N-G-O

B-I-N-G-O

And Bingo was his name, oh!

Many people repeat this verse five times, substituting a clap for one of the letters in Bingo's name (*clap*-I-N-G-O), and adding a clap each time, until the "B-I-N-G-O" line is just a series of five claps.

GAME

PLAY APPLE SNAP!

Charlotte begged Mama to let the children play Apple Snap, and Mama said they might.

Apple Snap

1. Tie a string around an apple and hang it from the ceiling, or a tree branch outside.
2. Without using their hands, players take turns trying to bite the apple.
3. The player who successfully bites the apple wins!

A variation on the game that's popular today is bobbing for apples. Here's how to play!

Bobbing for Apples

1. Float several apples in a tub of water.
2. Without using their hands, players take turns trying to remove an apple from the tub with their teeth.
3. The first one to successfully remove an apple wins!

RECIPE

Cornmeal Pudding with Molasses

Cornmeal pudding with molasses was Papa's very favorite of all the new foods he had learned to eat since he had come to America fifteen years ago. There was no molasses in Scotland, where he and Mama had grown up.

Now you can make cornmeal pudding, too!

½ CUP YELLOW CORNMEAL	MEASURING CUPS
4 CUPS MILK	BAKING DISH
1 CUP MOLASSES	DOUBLE BOILER
1 TEASPOON GINGER	SPOON
¼ TEASPOON SALT	

Note: Ask an adult for help with this recipe.

1. Mix the corn meal and milk together, and cook in a double boiler for half an hour.
2. Add the molasses, ginger, and salt.
3. Pour the mixture into a buttered baking dish.
4. Bake at 300 degrees for 3 hours.
5. Eat and enjoy!

ON TIDE MILL LANE

by MELISSA WILEY

THE CORNHUSKING

The great wide doors of Papa's blacksmith shop were shut and bolted. It was a sight that Charlotte had seldom seen, and normally it might feel a little strange. But tonight, a shiver of excitement ran through her. Papa had closed up early because Mr. John Heath was having a cornhusking.

"Whew!" said Papa. "Heath picked a cold night for it, didna he?"

"It'll be warm enough in his barn, with half the town there jawin'," Mama said. "Come, let's get over there before the baby takes a chill."

Mr. Heath's farm was just over the hill, across a stubbly hay meadow and an empty cornfield. All through August and September the farms around Roxbury had hummed with the work of harvesting. Now it was time for canning and preserving, husking and storing, making ready for the long, bitter winter. The air held the sharp smell of frost, and the leaves on the maples glowed a red orange as bright as Mama's hair.

Lewis ran ahead through the cornfield, leaping over the tilted stalks, intent on reaching the Heath place first.

"Last one there's a withered ear," he called back over his shoulder.

Tom sprinted to catch up. In his bulky woolen coat he looked stouter than ever, but he ran swift as a deer when he wanted to beat his older brother.

"I don't see why Tom bothers," Lydia said. "Imagine, a little child not yet eight beating a boy who's going on thirteen."

"Would you listen to that?" Mama teased,

"'A little child,' says she. I suppose you think you're quite an auld woman, Miss Lydia——— nine years old as you are."

Papa chuckled. "If she's an auld woman, that makes you ancient as the hills, Martha," he said.

"Ancient I may be, but I could still beat you in a footrace, Lew Tucker." Mama snorted, making the whole family laugh.

In the distance, they heard the din of Mr. Heath's barn, full of people.

Voices called out greetings to the Tucker family as they approached. Inside, the barn was noisy and warm. Miss Heath, Charlotte's teacher last summer, came up and kissed her cheek. She had pink cheeks and sparkling eyes, and her face was framed with long spiraling curls that had been made with a hot iron rod. Miss Heath did not seem much like a teacher now, whirling off to speak to another new arrival with her curls swinging out behind her, but Charlotte still felt honored for the kiss.

"She's Amelia tonight," Charlotte whispered.

"She's always Amelia," said Lydia, who had overheard. "That's her name."

Charlotte didn't try to explain. Lydia was not the sort of person to whom it was easy to explain things like your teacher having a "Miss Heath" self and an "Amelia" self.

The barn was crowded. On either side of a wide center walkway were great banks of hay stacked from floor to ceiling. Against one of the walls of hay was a mound, hundreds of unhusked ears of corn tumbled together. On the other side was a smaller pile of already husked corn, yellow as summer. The earthen floor in between was covered with a pale green carpet of discarded corn husks.

Small children ran this way and that, shuffling the corn husks with their feet. Grown-up men and women sat in groups on bales of hay, laughing as they stripped the leaves off the ears of corn. Boys dashed up to fling fine threads of corn silk into the hair of the girls who were busily fashioning dolls out of corn husks and thread.

Mama untied her cloak and set Mary down.

"Watch her, Charlotte," she called. Charlotte hurried after Mary, who was heading toward the great pile of corn. Mary came to the mountain of corn and crouched down; she took up an ear that was longer than her head and sank her teeth into the raw kernels.

"Mary, no!" Charlotte scolded, trying to wrestle the ear away. The grown-ups all around were chuckling as their hands flew over the ears of corn, stripping off the green leaves.

Mary was crying for her ear of corn. Charlotte put her arms around the baby's middle and carried her toward the girls making dolls. Lydia was there already. Tom and Lewis had disappeared into the mob of boys. There were so many people in the barn, it might as well have been a dance as a husking.

Across the barn a young man jumped onto a bale of hay with a fiddle on his shoulder. A cheer went up from the husking grown-ups. The young man had a wild head of hair cut short in the new fashion. He reminded Charlotte of Will, Papa's striker, who was faraway in the north, marching to Maine with the militia to defend the coast from the British. She wondered why the fiddler had not gone to war, and guessed that perhaps he was not yet eighteen years old. You had to be eighteen to serve in the militia. Charlotte's insides shivered with the cold feeling that came whenever she thought about the war and Will's being gone.

LITTLE HOUSE. BIG ADVENTURE.

Little House in the Highlands

It's 1788, and Martha lives in a little stone house in Glencaraid, Scotland. Martha's father is Laird Glencaraid, and the life of a laird's daughter is not always easy for a lively girl like Martha. She would rather be running barefoot through the fields of heather than acting like a proper lady! But between lessons, Martha always finds time to play on the rolling Scottish hills.

Little House by Boston Bay

It's 1814, and Charlotte lives with her family near the city of Boston. What an exciting time she has! There's Mama's garden to tend to, Papa's blacksmith shop to visit, and lots of brothers and sisters to play with. Best of all, Charlotte is a brand-new American girl, born just one generation after the United States of America was formed.

Little House in Brookfield

It's 1845, and Caroline Quiner lives in the bustling frontier town of Brookfield, Wisconsin. It's been one whole year since Caroline's father was lost at sea, and every member of her family must pitch in to help with the farm chores. With trips to town, getting through the first frost, and starting school, Caroline is busy discovering new things every day!

Little House on Rocky Ridge

It's 1893, and Rose and her parents, Laura and Almanzo, are moving to Missouri, the land of the Big Red Apple. They say goodbye to Ma and Pa Ingalls and Laura's sisters, and set off for the lush green valleys of the Ozarks. The journey is long and holds many adventures along the way, which they hope will lead them to a new home and a new life.